The Girl in the Torch

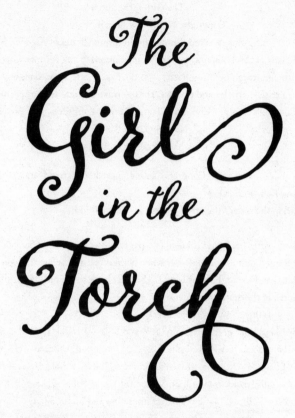

The Girl in the Torch

ROBERT SHARENOW

BALZER + BRAY
An Imprint of HarperCollins*Publishers*

Balzer + Bray is an imprint of HarperCollins Publishers.

The Girl in the Torch
Copyright © 2015 by Robert Sharenow

Library of Congress Cataloging-in-Publication Data
Sharenow, Rob, author.
The girl in the torch / Robert Sharenow. — First edition.
    pages cm
Summary: After her father is killed in a pogrom, twelve-year-old Sarah and her
mother immigrate to America—but when her mother dies before they get through
Ellis Island, and the authorities want to send her back to the old country, Sarah hides
in the torch of the Statue of Liberty.
    ISBN 978-0-06-222795-9 (hardcover)
    1. Ellis Island Immigration Station (N.Y. and N.J.)—Juvenile fiction. 2. Statue of
Liberty (New York, N.Y.)—Juvenile fiction. 3. Immigrant children—United States—
Juvenile fiction. 4. Orphans—Juvenile fiction. 5. Jews—United States—Juvenile
fiction. [1. Ellis Island Immigration Station (N.Y. and N.J.)—Fiction. 2. Statue of
Liberty (New York, N.Y.)—Fiction. 3. Emigration and immigration—Fiction.
4. Immigrants—Fiction. 5. Orphans—Fiction. 6. Jews—United States—Fiction.]
I. Author. II. Title.
PZ7.S52967 Gi 2015   2014030623
[Fic]—dc23   CIP
[813.6]   AC

Typography by Sarah Creech
15 16 17 18 19   CG/RRDH   10 9 8 7 6 5 4 3 2 1

First Edition

For Annabelle and Olivia

Contents

Here at our sea-washed, sunset gates shall stand
A mighty woman with a torch, whose flame
Is the imprisoned lightning, and her name
Mother of Exiles. From her beacon-hand
Glows world-wide welcome; her mild eyes command
The air-bridged harbor that twin cities frame.
"Keep, ancient lands, your storied pomp!" cries she
With silent lips. "Give me your tired, your poor,
Your huddled masses yearning to breathe free,
The wretched refuse of your teeming shore.
Send these, the homeless, tempest-tost to me,
I lift my lamp beside the golden door!"

—from Emma Lazarus, "The New Colossus," 1883

The Girl in the Torch

Horses

SARAH HEARD THE SOUND FIRST, a low rumble that she thought was thunder, gently rattling the windowpanes of their house like a shiver. The noise grew louder until she could tell it was hoofbeats, pounding down the dirt road that ran through their village as if one hundred angry drums were beating ever louder, ever closer. She pulled the blankets up so they almost covered her entire face and lay still in the dark, hoping they would pass. Finally the sound grew so loud that it woke her mother, who rolled over and shook Sarah's father. "Wake up!"

"Huh?" he mumbled, still half asleep.

They all slept in one room, the only room of the house, which was little more than four wooden walls, a thatched roof, and a floor. In the past year there had been other attacks, in other villages. So they knew what was happening.

"The horsemen," her mother said. "They're here!"

Her father sprang out of bed and pulled on his boots.

"Get into the root cellar," he said. "And don't come out no matter what."

"Papa . . . ?" Sarah sat up from the straw mat beside their bed.

"Don't question, Sarah," he said, grabbing her by the arm. "Just do as I say."

Though it was dark, she could see his eyes were hard and insistent. He turned from her, knocking into the table in the middle of the room. Sarah and her father had been in the middle of a chess match before bedtime and had left the board set up, frozen in midbattle. Now, he sent it flying into the air, scattering the carefully maneuvered pieces across the floor.

Sarah instinctively bent down to pick them up and reset the board, trying to recall what positions she had held and which of her father's pieces had been captured. But that thought was swept aside by her mother frantically pushing the table out of the way to get at the hatch of the root cellar that lay beneath it.

Her mother strained to move the heavy piece of furniture. "Help me," she gasped.

Sarah and her mother lifted the table while her father grabbed the pitchfork leaning against the wall near the door.

Her mother grasped his arm.

"Please don't go out there," she said.

He pulled away.

"You both stay here," he said, with a forceful, almost angry, authority that Sarah had never heard from him before. She had only known her father as a gentle man, a scholar, a buttonhole maker, not someone who yelled commands and used a pitchfork as a weapon. He looked at them and said, "Watch over each other.

And no matter what you hear, don't come out until they've gone."

Then he went outside.

Her mother paused, as if she were considering running after him. Then she locked the door from the inside with a wooden bar that she needed both arms to lift into place.

She pulled Sarah down into the small cellar that her husband had dug to store root vegetables and grain. Even in the chaos, something nagged at Sarah as her mother closed the door on top of them. *Ivan!* She bolted back into the room.

"What are you doing?" her mother shouted.

Sarah desperately felt around her blankets until her hand closed over the painted circus bear with a round belly and a silver hat with a pom-pom on top. Sarah's father had bought the carved wooden toy for her years ago from a traveling trinket salesman, and she had slept with it every night since. It was one of the only toys she had ever owned.

Sarah slipped Ivan into her pocket and returned to the cellar.

"Foolish girl," her mother hissed. Then she went silent.

They huddled together in the darkness, barely able to stand in the cramped space among the baskets of grain, carrots, and small yellow potatoes. The noises grew louder and more menacing: angry cries of attack, howls of pain, even some husky laughter. And always the hoofbeats. Five minutes. Ten minutes. Fifteen minutes passed with mother and daughter sweating inside the cellar, breathing air that became heavier and sourer as their anxiety rose.

Her mother ran her hands through Sarah's long red hair in an effort to soothe them both. Sarah squeezed Ivan in her skirt pocket.

Finally, after what seemed like hours, they heard the horses' thunder roll back down the dirt road away from the village. Sarah's mother waited another minute, her fingers digging into Sarah's shoulder. Then she sprang up out of the cellar, hoisted the wooden bar off the door, and ran outside.

Sarah gasped as the cold, sharp air stung her lungs, transforming her breath into puffs of steam as she trailed her mother into the center of town. A quarter moon lit the village in blue and black shadows. Dozens of men lay groaning on the ground, as other women and children tentatively emerged from their homes.

Her heartbeat quickened as her mother raced from man to man, looking for her father, calling his name at the dark lumps lying in the dirt. Finally, Sarah saw him, sitting up against a tree. She noticed his red beard first. They were the only two redheads in their village. He looked as if he was lying in a dark pool of oil, but as she got closer, a glint of moonlight struck the puddle, revealing a flash of crimson. It was only then that she noticed the pitchfork in his chest, as if he were a piece of paper tacked to the tree.

Her mother wailed and collapsed beside him, her nightdress soaking up the thick liquid as she unsuccessfully tried to shake him awake.

A horse with an empty saddle galloped through the center of town, trailing its reins behind. As Sarah stared at it, the chestnut-colored beast charged. It stopped short directly in front of her and reared up with a terrible growling neigh, its front hooves suspended high over Sarah's head. The girl stared into the snarling mouth of her certain death, her entire body frozen in terror.

And then she snapped awake.

Crossing

As Sarah's eyes shot open, she was greeted by darkness. She blinked once, twice, trying to bring the inside of her house into focus, but all she could see were more shades of black.

Then her body rolled to one side as the ship sharply crested a wave and she remembered that she and her mother were at sea.

Sarah heard the whir of the engine and the muffled breathing and sleep sounds of her fellow passengers. She felt around until she located Ivan safely tucked into the inner pocket of her coat. Her mother was lying beside her, breathing heavily, hot beneath the blankets and clothes they had stacked on top of themselves to keep warm.

The ship took another sharp dip, and her mother woke with a gasp.

"Sarah?" she called into the darkness.

"Yes, Mama."

"I need air. Come help me up."

Sarah reached under the covers to hoist her mother to her feet.

The woman's hands were warm and clammy, the blankets moist from her sweat.

Sarah led her mother over the other sleeping bodies and up the rusted iron ladder to the upper deck of the ship. Even though she was only twelve years old, Sarah was already tall enough to be able to carefully balance her mother against her shoulder to keep her upright.

The sight of the sea and the night sky, and the cool, salty October air filling her lungs, helped banish the memory of the nightmare. Her mother immediately ran to the side of the ship, gripped the railing, and violently sent most of her meager dinner overboard. Sarah recoiled; she couldn't recall her mother ever getting sick back in their village. A knot formed in the pit of her stomach.

Alone on deck, they stood in the quiet. Finally, her mother stepped back and drew a big breath. She steadied her hands on the railing, making sure there was nothing else coming up.

"Show me the Lady," her mother said. "That will make me feel better."

Sarah took a worn postcard from the pocket of her coat and handed it to her mother.

On the front of the card, a full moon peeked out from behind thick, dark clouds. The Lady stood in the semidarkness, towering over the harbor like a benevolent giant, holding her torch aloft with beams of light shining out as both a warning and an invitation. Beneath the starred crown, her expression was kind and proud all at once. Tiny trees and a flagpole surrounded her base. Sarah wondered if she could possibly be that big in real life.

She flipped over the card and read the words printed on the back, a poem that had been written about the Lady. Everyone in their village had been awed by the tantalizing message, as if it had been personally written for them.

"'Mother of Exiles . . . ,'" Sarah read. "'With silent lips. "Give me your tired, your poor, / Your huddled masses. . . . / I lift my lamp beside the golden door!"'"

"Let it be so," said her mother.

Sarah wondered if there ever had been more wonderful words written. Surely America would be different from their old country, where her people were barely allowed to live, never mind be welcomed in the way that was promised in the poem.

Sarah's mother could not read or write, yet Sarah had been taught to do both by her father.

"Why bother?" one of her father's friends had asked. "Does a girl need to read to milk a cow or boil a chicken?"

"My girl's mind is as sharp as any of your sons'," her father said. "So why not?"

Sarah's parents had been planning their escape to America for two years before the attack on their village. To prepare for their new life, Sarah had been studying English with the son of the village wool merchant, who was a university student. It was Sarah who had first translated the poem on the postcard and read it to her amazed family and neighbors. The card had been sent by her father's sister, who had moved to the United States nearly ten years earlier.

She held up the postcard against the night sky, trying to fit the image into the real horizon. She lined up the picture so it was just right, and her mother smiled and started to sing. Although she had never gone to school, her mother had a gift for melody and song. She improvised countless little tunes throughout the day— lullabies, work songs—to amuse them.

Have you ever seen a golden door?
So bright it makes your eyes feel sore.
Good luck spills across the floor
In the room behind the golden door,
The golden door. The golden door.

The lyrics came alive in Sarah's mind with images of golden doors and streets paved with riches. Sarah imagined them living in a perfect little house along one of those streets with plenty of food to eat and peaceful neighbors. When her mother's stomach felt settled enough, they returned belowdecks.

The next night, Sarah's mother woke her again. This time, she barely made it to the railing before vomiting over the side. But unlike the previous night, it brought no relief.

She asked Sarah to hold the postcard up to the horizon once more.

"If we do this every night, maybe the real Lady will appear

sooner," her mother said weakly. Sarah sent up a silent prayer to make it so.

The next day, her mother's fever didn't break. She told Sarah that she was just seasick, that they weren't seafaring folk.

"I'll never get used to living in a room with floors that move beneath my feet," she said. "That's all it is."

Worries whirled in Sarah's mind. She had found her sea legs days earlier. But she didn't argue. She just worried to herself.

A Widening Circle

THE FOLLOWING MORNING, HER mother wasn't even able to get up the ladder before dizziness overwhelmed her and she was forced to go back and lie down. Sarah had to fetch a bucket and empty it over the side throughout the day and night. She constantly felt her mother's forehead. Her fever grew higher and higher until her face felt like the side of a boiling teakettle.

There was a couple on board who had come from a village very near their own and were traveling with their infant son. Earlier in the trip, Sarah's mother had made conversation with them about people they knew in common and what their plans were for the New World. Now Sarah approached them.

"Excuse me," she said.

"Please, stay back," the husband said, holding up his hand and placing his body between Sarah and his wife and child.

"Please," Sarah said. "My mother's fever won't break. And she's not making sense when she talks."

"Look, I really can't help you. I'm not a doctor. I can't risk my wife or baby catching her illness. I'm sorry."

Sarah retreated to her corner.

The next night, Sarah made another trip to the top deck to empty her mother's bucket. It was moments before dawn; the bottom of the sky was just beginning to lighten, a pale gray and yellow border on black. A group of large gulls dived after her mother's waste as Sarah poured it over the side.

Glancing up, she saw dozens of the birds as they cawed and screeched and fluttered around the ship. She looked out through the waning darkness and saw another steamship, then a long wooden sailboat with two masts, and several small fishing boats. As the sky lightened, she could see more birds and boats appearing out of the darkness around her.

And then she saw her in the far distance. Sarah had looked at the postcard so many times that she knew the Lady immediately, by just the faintest suggestion of her silhouette. The sun came creeping over the horizon and the ship moved them closer and closer. Sarah stared, transfixed, as the statue came into sharper focus.

Another passenger, a thin man with a scraggly beard, appeared behind her from below. He froze in his tracks, his eyes went wide, and he yelled, "WE'RE HERE!"

The Golden Door

Most of the other passengers stirred and joined them on deck, excitedly pointing and cheering at the sight of the Lady.

"Thank the Lord!"

"America!"

Some broke into song. Others cried. One couple hugged each other so tightly, Sarah thought they might never let go. Some literally danced for joy.

Swept up in the moment, Sarah found herself clapping along, her legs kicking and jumping in place as if she could leap over the water to the promised land.

As the statue came closer, Sarah slipped the postcard out of her pocket. The actual Lady was far more beautiful and majestic than could ever be captured in a picture. So many new details came alive as she stared at the real thing, from the Lady's thick parted hair beneath the crown to the angular lines of her neck to the muscular firmness of her torch-bearing arm. Sarah let out a small gasp of delight as she saw the faces of several people inside the windows in the crown. She removed Ivan from her pocket.

"Look, Ivan," she said. "There she is."

More people came on deck, until it seemed as if everyone on board must have been standing at the railing cheering and watching the New World come into view. She saw a young mother holding a baby swaddled in a blanket.

"It's our new home," the woman said to her baby.

The sight of the young mother made Sarah remember her own. She shoved Ivan into her pocket, feeling guilty for having shown her toy bear the New World first. Sarah rushed back down into the hold and found her mother lying in a fevered sleep, a small lump in the middle of the otherwise deserted room.

"Mama, wake up! We're here. We're finally here!"

Her mother's skin burned, but her eyes fluttered open and she muttered, "Thank God. Thank God."

The other passengers began to trickle back belowdecks to pack up their belongings and discuss plans for their arrival. One woman, another mother, who traveled with her husband and two children, walked up to Sarah. It was the first time in days that anyone besides her mother had talked to her.

"You must try to make your mother look well," the woman said.

"What do you mean?" said Sarah.

"They don't let in the sick. If you don't make her look well, they won't let her in."

Make her look well? But how? Sarah wet a cloth and wiped her mother's face, her neck, and under her arms, which revived her a bit. Sarah combed her hair and straightened her clothes as best she could. Eventually she was able to get her to stand and coaxed her up the ladder.

A sharp orange sun had risen into the cloudless sky, and they both had to squint as they came up onto the deck. Sarah led her to the railing.

"Look, Mama. There she is."

Now just a few hundred yards away, the Lady's face beamed down at them, silent and strong. Sarah's mother smiled and whispered, "Thank the Lord."

The ship sailed deeper into the harbor, until the Lady loomed over them and Sarah could see scores of people milling around at her base and up inside her torch and crown. She gasped in wonder, longing to be on the island, to explore inside the Lady and see the view from the windows of the crown and the walkway of the torch.

As they moved beyond the statue, Sarah saw New York City come into focus, the tip of Manhattan packed with buildings more tightly than she had ever thought possible, stretching into the distance as far as the eye could see. It was as if someone had stacked hundreds of villages on top of one another. Boats of all shapes and sizes moved around the island.

"Isn't it incredible, Mama?" Sarah asked.

But her mother didn't respond. Her eyes were glazed over and she seemed to be staring at nothing in particular.

The ship banked sharply to the left and docked at a small island behind the Lady. A large building that looked like a castle or fortress dominated the shoreline. The main building had four towers with rounded roofs that looked like onions.

The passengers gathered their belongings, all jostling to be the first to disembark. A line of men waited for them on the dock. They wore uniforms with stiff round blue hats and badges.

Sarah struggled to carry their few belongings and to help her mother off the ship. Once on shore, they lined up to enter the main building, and Sarah felt a pinch of disappointment as she saw that the entry door was not actually made of gold, but was wooden like any other door. She reached out and ran her finger along the dull surface. What other disappointments would she find here? Sarah wondered.

They waited outside for a half hour, and Sarah and the other passengers' excitement turned to impatience.

"It's nice to know that some things are the same as the old country," one man joked. "I guess all governments are good at making people wait in lines."

A few of the others laughed, but as the minutes ticked by, the tension rose and the crowd fell quiet. Her mother sat on one of their bags, holding her head in her hands. Finally, an official came out to usher them inside. Sarah hoisted her mother to her feet and they stepped into the building.

Sarah gasped and stopped short.

Quarantine

THEY ENTERED A MASSIVE main hall filled with hundreds of people just like the passengers from her ship, waiting in several different lines that snaked through the room. The lines were separated by a series of rigid metal posts and ropes just like the rows of cattle pens in the slaughterhouse on the outskirts of her village.

The air vibrated with the sound of dozens of languages being spoken all at once. Sarah looked up and down the lines. She could hardly believe that human beings could come in so many different shapes and sizes. Short, tall, fat, skinny, ugly, beautiful, old, young, crippled, strong, brown haired, black haired, blond haired, even some redheads like her.

Some men wore beards while others were completely clean-shaven and looked more like boys than men. Some dressed in Old World clothes with baggy pants tucked into high socks, white shirts with puffy white sleeves, and strange hats shaped like large red cups. Still others wore neat modern three-piece suits and bowler hats. Some women had their hair tucked under kerchiefs and wore long, plain, heavy black dresses. Others had their hair piled up in fancy arrangements held together by jeweled pins and wore bright dresses, with corsets pulling in their waists and pushing up their bosoms so that they indelicately spilled over the tops of their blouses.

Sarah was also transfixed by the men in uniform and the other people working in the building. Beneath their similar dress, there was an amazing array of skin tones, from the palest white to the darkest brown and everything in between. Nearly everyone at home had looked the same, with dark hair and dark eyes and similar clothes.

Sarah and the other passengers were led to the medical examination area, where groups of doctors and officials carrying clipboards and chalk made quick evaluations of the immigrants on line.

"Who are they?" a woman asked her husband.

"I think it must be the medical people. I heard they examine everyone as soon as they come ashore to make sure everyone's healthy."

Sarah's entire body tightened with concern as she watched the exams from a distance. The doctors made very quick judgments. Most people were allowed to pass, although several were marked with a letter in chalk on their clothing and led away.

The jagged line of passengers from Sarah's ship chattered excitedly to one another. Sarah and her mother stood at the very end, a few yards away from the next-to-last person. Sarah nervously shuffled in place, measuring the distance the others were keeping from them and worrying that the officials would notice and assume the worst.

At last it was their turn. One of the men in uniform spoke some Yiddish and Russian and asked them their names and where they came from. Her mother attempted to answer the questions as best she could, while the doctor examined Sarah.

Sarah gagged as he roughly pressed down her tongue with a dry wooden stick. He poked and prodded her body with his hands and medical instruments. Finally he took out a small metal buttonhook and reached it toward her eye. Sarah flinched and tried to turn away.

"Hold still," he commanded as he pulled back the skin of her eye with the instrument and examined each eyeball.

"She looks fine," he said.

As soon as the doctor turned his attention to her mother, though, his expression changed. He stared into her eyes, clearly not liking what he saw in their glassy yellow reflection. He took her mother's temperature and pulse; and then the men stepped away to confer for a moment. Sarah's mother slumped against the girl's shoulder.

Finally the Yiddish-speaking official returned and abruptly drew a large letter *P* on her mother's coat near the shoulder with a thick piece of chalk.

"What is this about?" Sarah's mother asked.

"I'm afraid you're not well. The *P* stands for physical and lungs. We think you have some sort of physical illness or infection," the man said. "We're going to have to take you for treatment at our hospital while your daughter proceeds to the processing center."

"But I need to get to the United States," her mother said.

"It's in the United States," the man said. "It's just in another area of the facility."

"Why can't we stay together?" her mother asked.

"Your daughter is healthy. We need to keep you quarantined so you don't get anyone else sick, including her. She'll be perfectly safe."

The word *quarantined* sent a chill down Sarah's spine, even though she wasn't quite sure what it meant.

"I'm afraid you don't have any choice in the matter. We have a wonderful hospital, and I'm sure you will get better and be on your way in no time."

He turned away to deal with the other passengers on line, and another official gestured for Sarah's mother to come with him.

Sarah's throat went dry.

"Mama . . ."

"We don't have a choice, little one," she said, shaking her head.

"But I can't be alone."

"Let's move it along," the official said.

"One minute," Sarah's mother told him.

Mustering her remaining strength, her mother knelt before Sarah.

"You will be fine," she said. "We both will be. You are my brave, beautiful girl. American doctors are the best in the world.

They will make me well, and then we will enter the New World together. Promise me you'll be strong."

Sarah just stared at her.

"Promise me," her mother insisted.

"I promise," Sarah finally said, wishing she believed it.

Sarah's mother kissed her on the head one final time and then was led away. She turned and waved to Sarah, barely able to find the strength to hold up her arm, then blew her a final kiss. Then she rounded a corner and was gone. Sarah was alone.

Sarah's anxiety rose as she waited for another hour until she finally made it to the front of the next line and approached a man in uniform, sitting in an elevated booth.

"How old are you?" he asked in Yiddish.

"Twelve," she replied.

"Twelve? I would've guessed you were at least fifteen. I have a sixteen-year-old girl, and she's much younger looking than you. But I guess that's a good thing, because she can't push me around as easily."

He chuckled. It made Sarah feel good that the official thought she was older.

"Do you know a trade?" he asked.

"My mother and I are both buttonhole makers," Sarah said.

He nodded. "It's good to have a skill."

Sarah's father had taught both of them the basic skills of buttonhole making, although they didn't possess anywhere near his expertise. She did have his one pair of fine professional scissors, the most valuable possession they had carried with them from the old country. Her mother had sewn a special pocket for them inside Sarah's jacket.

"Now, we're going to have to hold you here in the dormitory while your mother gets well. That is, unless you have American relations who can come pick you up. Do you have relatives here?"

"My father's sister and her family."

Sarah had never met her aunt, whose family had moved to Germany before settling in the United States.

"And are they in New York?" the man asked.

"They live somewhere called Brook-a-lin."

"Brooklyn is a part of New York." He smiled.

"I have their name and address here." She handed the man the piece of paper that her mother had given her to hold. It said:

Cohen. Brookalin. New York. United State.

The official gave her back the piece of paper.

"There are hundreds, maybe thousands of families named Cohen in Brooklyn," he said. "Do you have any more information?"

"My aunt's name is Rivka."

"Okay. It's not much to go on, but we'll try to contact them."

"May I visit my mother now?" Sarah asked hopefully.

The man's expression turned more serious.

"She has to be given a clean bill of health before she can see anyone, but don't worry. She'll be well taken care of, and you'll be in a nice safe place until she's better."

Sarah was led to a dormitory building and given a bed in a large room filled with other women and girls who were also being detained for one reason or another. Most of the others were groups: mothers and daughters, sets of sisters, or just friends who had made the journey together. Scanning the room, she realized she was one of the few who were alone.

Volunteering

THAT NIGHT, SARAH TRIED to sleep, but after so many days at sea it felt as if the building was moving like the ship. With Ivan tucked beneath the blanket beside her, Sarah stared at the high-beamed ceiling and listened to everyone breathing in the darkness. *I guess everyone snores in the same language,* she thought.

Closing her eyes, she whispered a prayer for her mother, hoping that she would be able to share everything with her tomorrow.

Yet for the next two days the officials told her that her mother was still being treated at the hospital. On the third day, she found her way to the roof garden, a large, fenced-in outdoor area on top of the dormitory building that buzzed with activity.

In one corner little children climbed all over a set of swings, a seesaw, and a pair of slides. Sarah had never seen a playground before, so she was shocked to watch the children bouncing, sliding, and flying through the air. Even though most of them spoke different languages, they played together easily, joining into groups, laughing and chasing each other.

On the opposite side of the roof, several American women were leading classes for older immigrant children. One group was being instructed on the basics of how to sew and the other was being given a rudimentary English lesson.

A woman with thick brown hair arranged in a bun stood before a chalkboard and wrote out the alphabet, explaining the pronunciation of each letter.

"This is the letter *B*," the woman explained. "It's pronounced *bee*. Say it after me: *B*."

The class repeated the letter. Sarah inched closer until the teacher noticed her.

"Would you like to join one of the classes?"

"Oh, I know how to speak and write English and sew," Sarah said with some pride.

"I suppose you do," the woman said, impressed. "I'm Miss O'Connell. Maybe you'd like to help our other volunteers with the younger children." She gestured toward the other side of the roof, where a few young women were helping to organize the children into games. "They could use an extra set of hands."

Sarah nodded.

Sarah spent the morning assisting the other women as they corralled the small children into races and games of tag and ring-around-the-rosy. At noon she helped lead them to the cafeteria and fed some of the littlest ones in between eating her own sandwich. Sarah liked working with the children and blending in with the other volunteers, and the hours flew by.

At the end of the day, Miss O'Connell had each child line up and shake hands and say thank you to all the volunteers. When the final child was gone, Sarah helped to clean up.

"Thanks for your help," Miss O'Connell said to Sarah. "Maybe you can come back and help me again sometime."

"I'm waiting for my mother to get out of the hospital, so I will not be here much longer."

Sarah tried to say this with confidence, but she couldn't help but feel a gnawing sense of doubt.

"Of course," Miss O'Connell said. "Good luck to you."

As Sarah returned to the dormitory, her mind raced with excited thoughts about the future. Maybe she would be a teacher instead of a buttonhole maker. Or maybe she'd become something else, something she hadn't yet imagined. America seemed filled with possibilities.

Passed

THE NEXT MORNING, A NURSE ARRIVED at Sarah's bedside, accompanied by another woman wearing a plain blue skirt and blouse. The nurse carried a cinnamon bun with powdered sugar sprinkled on top and her face wore a serious, sad expression. Sarah's stomach dropped.

The woman in the blue skirt sat down on Sarah's cot and handed her the bun. The nurse stood above them both.

"I'm afraid that I have some bad news," the woman said. "The doctors tried as best they could to help your mother. But there was nothing they could do. She passed in the night."

"Passed?"

At first, Sarah didn't fully understand what the woman was saying. Passed where? Or passed what? Had she passed the medical examination that would allow them to leave? Had she passed on to New York City without her?

"Her fever wouldn't break. And she didn't respond to the medicine. They tried everything. But the illness had progressed too far."

Sarah tried to catch up with the dark, unfamiliar words.

"She had to be buried right away, because of her disease, to keep it from spreading."

"Buried," Sarah repeated.

"Yes," the official confirmed. "I'm terribly sorry."

She continued talking, but Sarah could no longer hear her. All of the woman's words seemed to scramble and blend into a low hum. Her body felt heavy and numb, sinking into the cloth of the cot as if it were quicksand. Her breath pulsed out of her mouth in desperate little heaves.

Until the quarantine, not a day of Sarah's life had passed by without seeing her mother, without spending most of every waking hour beside her. And now, she was gone.

Sarah tried to picture her, but it was as if all her memories had floated up to heaven along with her mother's spirit. She could more easily imagine her father's face, his red hair and beard, the deep crow's-feet that formed around his eyes whenever he was pleased about something. She imagined her mother's long thin legs, her brown hair, the faded freckles over the bridge of her nose, but they refused to come together to form a distinct whole.

"Mama?"

"She's gone, dear."

"Mama?" Her voice rose in pitch.

"I'm sorry."

"Mama!" Sarah called again, knowing it would go unanswered.

The nurse sat beside her and tried to lay a consoling hand on her back, but Sarah recoiled and curled into herself, hugging her legs.

Suddenly a word came into her head that was so terrifying, it blotted out everything else. *Orphan.* Growing up, she had heard horrible stories about orphanages, where children without parents were forced to work at hard labor all day to earn their keep, and those who didn't were starved or beaten to death.

The word snapped Sarah back to the present.

"What will happen to me?"

"We're still trying to find your relatives in Brooklyn," the official said. "We put notices in the Brooklyn newspapers, but it might take some time."

The official said this with an air of confidence that made Sarah think that they dealt with girls in her situation all the time.

"What if you can't find them?"

The woman looked at the nurse.

"Let's give it some more time," she said. "Again, we're very sorry for your loss."

The woman and the nurse walked away.

Sarah looked at the cinnamon bun in her hand. The idea of food made her feel sick. She tried to imagine what her mother might say to calm her down, but she couldn't even remember what her voice had sounded like.

The only memory that formed in Sarah's mind was of her mother standing at their table chopping vegetables with a distinct rhythm, chop, chop, chop, chop, one, two, three, four, chop, chop,

chop, chop, one, two, three, four, in a steady beat. Her mother would hum or make up a tune along with the rhythm of the chopping. She must have made up hundreds, maybe thousands of funny little songs while she cooked. Yet Sarah couldn't recall a single one.

How could a person who just days before had been so solid and sure become just a cloudy image, just a wisp of a song?

That night Sarah stared into the high-beamed ceiling of the darkened dormitory and tried to see through it to the sky. She imagined her mother's spirit in the moonlit clouds, ascending to the other world where her father would be waiting.

Before closing her eyes, Sarah prayed for her mother's safe delivery to heaven. But she prayed even harder for the officials to find her relatives, or for them to find her.

Uncle Jossel

SEVERAL DAYS PASSED AND still no word came about her aunt in Brooklyn. Everyone in the dormitory who Sarah had arrived with had departed. Weighed down by the sadness of losing her mother, she couldn't bring herself to return to the roof garden to assist Miss O'Connell. She spent most of her time wandering the grounds alone, watching people come and go, worrying and waiting.

Each day, one of the friendly officials would give her his newspaper when he was done, so she could practice her English. She would sit on a bench outside and read every word, from cover to cover, soaking up as much news of America as she could, to prepare for when the Cohens would take her to live with them in Brooklyn.

One afternoon, after a full week of waiting, Sarah was resting on her bed when the woman in the blue skirt came to visit with a male official.

"I'm afraid we weren't able to find your family," the woman said.

"What do you mean, you couldn't find them?"

"We tracked down their last known address, but the landlord of the building said they moved a year ago."

"A year ago?" Sarah repeated, panic rising in her chest. "Can't you keep looking?"

"He said they moved somewhere out in the western part of the country. He didn't even know the state. I'm sorry."

"What's going to happen to me?" Sarah asked.

"Our records indicate that you have an uncle back in your old country. Your mother's brother."

"Uncle Jossel?"

"Yes."

"But I don't know him very well."

"That's okay." The woman nodded reassuringly. "A blood relation is a blood relation."

Sarah wasn't sure exactly what the woman meant, but her heart sank. Her uncle was a bachelor who lived in a nearby village. He was very heavyset and wore glasses and had a long bushy beard with gray curls. Whenever he visited, he refused to directly address her, or her mother for that matter.

"Tell the girl to fetch us some water from the well," he would call to her mother without giving either of them a glance. Then later, "Tell the girl to come clear our cups. And be quick about it."

"He doesn't even look at me when he gives orders," she said to her mother. "It's like I'm not even there."

"My brother believes that men have their world, and women

and girls have theirs. And he likes to keep it that way."

"Well, I don't," Sarah said.

The memory made Sarah feel sick to her stomach. How could she remember the details of her detested uncle and hear his deep, wheezy voice more clearly than she could her own mother?

"Isn't there any way I could stay?" Sarah asked the official.

"With no relatives, you'd be a public charge," the man said.

"What does that mean?"

"That means the state would have to pay to support you, and you'd likely be sent to an orphanage. It's better if you go back. I'm sure your uncle will be more than happy to take you in," the official said.

Sarah knew he would not be. "Has anyone written to my uncle to see if he wants me?"

"Someone in your country will help track him down for you," the man said.

"But he doesn't like children or girls," Sarah pleaded. She had to make them understand. "What if he doesn't want to take me?"

"I'm sure he will," the woman answered.

"But what if he doesn't?"

"I'm sure they'll be able to take care of you in your own country."

My own country? Sarah thought. *That place isn't my country. My people aren't welcome there. Our village was attacked. That's why we came here in the first place.*

But her jaw tightened shut.

The official explained that her passage had been booked on a ship that left that very evening. Sarah watched them walk away and pass beneath the American flag that hung over the door. She stared at the flag's rich red stripes and the blue square covered with stars, the reality sinking in. They were Americans. She was not. She would never step through the golden door.

Salt Water

THE NIGHT WAS COOL AND CLEAR as the ship pulled out into New York harbor. A chilling October breeze blew Sarah's red hair as she stood on the back deck of the ship staring at the yellow lights of Manhattan passing behind her like a glittering fantasyland that would now only exist in stories for her, no different from a fairy-tale kingdom. She thought of the thousands of people rushing around on that island, thousands of families, but none who belonged to her. Sarah sat cross-legged, looking between the bars of the railing into the black water below. The other passengers were belowdecks, settling in for the late-night voyage, so she was alone.

She took Ivan out of her pocket and set him up on the deck next to her so he could see New York City one last time.

"Say good-bye, little friend," she whispered.

As the Lady came into view, Sarah turned to the front of the ship. The light of the torch shone through the darkness, no longer a signal of welcome but just a warning to passing ships to avoid smashing onto the rocks of the island. She took out the postcard of the Lady and held it up against the horizon line just as she had on the journey over.

Looking at the postcard triggered something in Sarah. The image of her mother standing on deck during their voyage rushed into her mind—her face, her posture, the sound of her voice. Memories came back to Sarah all at once, from their journey to America, her childhood, from her entire life. Hundreds of distinct little moments, gestures, expressions, and songs that pricked her like pins: tying a dark-green ribbon in Sarah's hair, trimming her father's beard, washing her arms and neck in their metal basin, milking the family goat in the backyard, singing lullabies at night.

A single word rose up from Sarah's belly and escaped her lips.

"Mama . . ."

The sound was instantly swallowed by the noise of the water and the ship. A deep wound throbbed inside her where the word had come from, where her mother's presence had been ripped away. She closed her eyes to stop the memories, but they only came faster. Tears broke from beneath Sarah's lids, running down her face and into the sea, salt water mixing with salt water.

But then her sadness gave way as anger bubbled up inside her. She was angry at the immigration officials for sending her home, at her relatives for moving west without telling anyone, at her uncle for being so awful. Even at her parents for leaving her alone in the world.

In a burst of frustration, Sarah tore the postcard in half, shocking herself that she could destroy something that had once been so precious. She ripped the two halves into smaller pieces, tossing them into the water below. She leaned forward, trying to see them, but couldn't make out anything in the choppy black sea.

"Good-bye, America," she whispered.

Staring into the darkness, Sarah realized that she had nothing left. No family. No hopes. Nothing. Everything good she possibly could think of was in her past. The golden door had been permanently shut.

Then she glanced back up at the Lady, her face so strong and beautiful. Sarah and her mother had looked at the postcard so many times, dreaming of seeing her in person, and of the life they would lead in America.

Sarah felt a small spark inside her at the memory.

She balled her hands into tight fists.

"We can't go back there," she muttered, gripping Ivan. "We won't go back."

Sarah gazed at Manhattan.

When she was a little girl, Sarah's father taught her to swim in a small pond near their village. Like reading and writing, learning how to swim was unusual for a girl in her village, but her father had always insisted that she learn whatever he could teach.

"If I could teach you to fly, I'd do that too," he explained. "But I haven't perfected that myself . . . yet."

He laughed a big laugh. Her mother thought they were both crazy and sang the same song every time they headed out for a lesson.

My husband has the strangest wish
To turn our daughter to a fish.
Every day I hear him shout,
"Look, there goes my little trout."

Sarah's eyes focused on the glittering lights of the promised land in the distance. She had never attempted to swim anywhere near that far. *Could I make it?* she wondered.

She had to try.

Sarah stood up, shoved the toy bear back into her pocket, and glanced around the deck. There was no one in sight. She climbed up onto the railing and hoisted herself over the top, perching on the outer edge, just barely dangling above the water below. She had no idea how far down the water was, but she tried to measure how many of her body lengths it was and stopped counting when she reached seven, which meant that it was nearly forty feet.

Sarah stared at the Lady, trying to gather her courage.

Finally she closed her eyes.

One. Two. Three!

Sarah let go of the railing and stepped off into the night. She held her breath tightly, and her body fell through the air for what seemed like an eternity. She was just running out of breath and about to open her mouth for another when she hit the surface with a hard slap.

She plunged feetfirst into the cold black water, her entire body stinging from the icy impact, her mouth and nose filling with the ocean. Her body convulsed as the water struck the back of her nose, her throat, her lungs. She coughed an angry mouthful of bubbles into the dense blackness. The voice of her father flooded into her head, as loud and clear as any memory had ever been.

"Never try to breathe underwater. You're not a herring, little one."

Sarah frantically pulled herself up, pumping her arms and kicking her legs with all the energy she could muster. Her lungs ached and she felt her mouth and nose struggling to resist the instinct to open and take something in. One more breath of salt water would fill her lungs and drag her down.

Despite the freezing water, her insides started to burn and her head tingled as her stomach and chest muscles contracted to squeeze out any remaining oxygen. Just as she felt that she couldn't make it another inch, she broke the surface and gulped a huge breath of night air. She coughed and spit seawater, which kept slapping in and out of her mouth in small waves that moved around her.

Sarah bobbed on the surface, trying to get her bearings. The ship loomed above her, a huge black shadow against the night sky, quickly moving farther out toward the open sea. The violent force of a wave caused by the vessel's massive propellers pushed her back and down. She held her breath as she was pulled underwater in the great churn.

Night Swimming

SARAH FIERCELY KICKED HER legs to resurface. Another wave and she was smacked back down and dragged under by more violent rushes of water. She paddled and pulled herself back up into the air, gulping in as much oxygen as possible to prepare herself for another fight beneath the waves.

But the water had calmed enough that she could ride atop the waves instead of being pulled below them. As the ship moved farther away, the waves subsided until Sarah was treading water in the normal ebb and flow of the harbor, and she was finally able to unclench her body and catch her breath. She floated on her back and gazed up into a sky filled with bright stars and shadowy clouds passing before the moon.

In the stillness, she finally felt the soreness of her arms and legs, which had been bruised when she hit the water. Patches of skin along her shins and forearms were raised in angry red welts that were painful to the touch. She moved her limbs. Thank goodness nothing had been broken.

Wait! Where's Ivan?

She patted down all her pockets. They were empty.

"Ivan!" she called into the darkness as if he could hear. She scooped handfuls of the dark water around her, her panic rising. She looked around her but could see almost nothing clearly on the rippling surface of the water. She called out to him again.

"Ivan!"

She swam with her hands outstretched, searching the water around her, feeling in and around the waves. But all she touched were a few strands of slimy seaweed. Finally, off in the distance, she saw a glint of silver bobbing in the water. Could it be the paint of his hat? The glint disappeared under a wave, but Sarah dived toward it, moving her hands through the water until finally they touched something. It slipped away under another wave, but then she grabbed into the water and her hand fell around the bear. She held him tightly to her chest.

"Don't swim away like that again."

Sarah gripped Ivan in her hand and floated on her back to catch her breath. She had only been resting for a minute when an icy chill soaked her skin and sharp gooseflesh sprouted across her body.

She had to keep moving or she'd freeze to death.

She considered taking off her high-laced boots but feared that it would take too long to remove them. Stripping off her coat, she struggled to say afloat as she tied it tightly around her waist so she could more easily move her arms. Sarah treaded water to get her bearings and saw New York way off in the distance. It had looked so much closer from the ship. She could never make it that far.

Looking around her, she caught sight of the Lady's glowing torch. The statue's small island was just a few hundred yards away. She fixed her eyes on the torch and started to swim toward it, remembering her father's instruction to kick her legs like a frog and move her arms like she was opening a set of curtains, over and over in a steady rhythm. Up, out, together, glide. Up, out, together, glide.

The movement stirred her blood, fighting off the cold. It was difficult to swim with Ivan clutched in her fist, but she couldn't risk putting him back in her pocket.

Sarah shuddered as something slithered against her leg. A moment later, something else brushed her foot. She paddled and kicked faster, too afraid to slow down and try to swat or kick the creatures away. She tried not to think of what might be swimming with her.

She had to rest every few minutes, only allowing herself to float until she felt the cold creeping across her flesh. She made gradual progress, always keeping the Lady and the torch in her sights.

Her legs and arms felt heavier and heavier, and just keeping herself afloat was sapping all of her strength. She tried to rest by floating on her back, but whenever she did, the cold overtook her and waves lapped on top of her, soaking her face and stinging her eyes.

Sarah was lying on her back when—*thud!*—something hard hit the back of her head.

She gasped in pain.

Spinning around in the water, Sarah discovered a large wooden pallet. It must have floated away from the mainland.

She maneuvered the top of her body onto the pallet like it was a life raft and then used her legs to kick toward the island.

The poem about the Lady ran through her mind, as if its lines were words of encouragement written specifically for her right now. "Give me your tired, your poor, / . . . The wretched refuse of your teeming shore. / Send these, the homeless, tempest-tost to me."

Finally the shadowy outline of the island's rocky shore came into view. *Keep kicking. Just a little more,* she told herself.

When she was a few yards from shore, her knee cracked against the side of a rock. The sting was sharp and she knew the blow had broken skin. She let go of her raft and felt her way toward shore. Her hand touched another rock but slipped off.

Reaching into the dark water, she grabbed onto the rock again and pulled herself to it. She rested, holding it for a moment, before venturing forward to the next. Sarah cautiously floated from rock to rock, feeling around with her hands, until she was able to haul herself up and out of the water and onto something dry.

She crawled a few feet until she felt grass under her sore knees. Her heart pounded and her muscles tingled with exhaustion and relief as she flipped over onto her back and stared into the sky, her chest heaving, taking in huge mouthfuls of night air.

Sarah rolled over onto her side and then hauled herself up and onto her knees. She had come ashore on the west side of the island, the back of the Lady towering over her. The Lady's massive right foot stuck out of the back of her robe, as if she was striding forward, a small detail Sarah had never known existed.

Taking a deep breath, Sarah stood up. She needed to see the Lady from the front, to come face-to-face with her. So she picked herself up, shoved Ivan into her pocket, and ran to the front of the island, until finally the Lady's magnificent gaze fell upon her.

And it was just the two of them alone, staring at each other. Sarah was awed by the Lady's face lit by moonlight, a face that she had only dreamed about, seen in photographs and drawings, or from a distance. Her eyes were calm but strong, her lips perfectly formed, her nose straight and broad, her hair neatly parted in the middle and tucked under her crown. The Lady was so close and so real, Sarah began to laugh with joy at being alone with such a wondrous thing.

As her laughter subsided, she noticed the absolute quiet of the island. The water lapping against the rocky shore was the only sound. She scanned the landscape, struck by how strange it felt to be in such a wide-open space with no other people, particularly after the overcrowding of the ship and Ellis Island. She listened to the sound of her own breath mingling with the gentle lapping of the waves and the wind.

Suddenly she heard the sharp noise of breaking glass and a deep, hacking cough.

She wasn't alone.

The Watchman

SARAH STUFFED IVAN INTO her pocket and scurried across the grass, trying to keep herself as low to the ground as possible. With her head tucked down so that her red hair wouldn't shine in the moonlight and give her away, she crept toward a small clump of trees that stood in a row behind the Lady's enormous base. There was another deep cough, but Sarah was afraid to stop and find exactly where the sound was coming from.

Reaching the trees, she wrapped herself around the nearest trunk and scanned the island, but couldn't see anyone. The tree, a large oak filled with leaves that had already lost their green in the fall chill, had several low-hanging branches. Sarah grabbed for the lowest one and pulled herself up into the leafy cover. She carefully climbed through thick branches until she was about halfway up and could look out onto the clearing. At first, she saw nothing. Then she heard another cough.

Off in the distance, about fifty yards away, Sarah spied a dark lump on the path that led away from the base of the Lady. As the lump moved and coughed again, she could make out the faint outline of a man on his hands and knees. A small lantern sat beside him, glowing a dull thin yellow line of kerosene flame. The man arched his back and spit a deep lungful of phlegm onto the ground. Then he rose, first with hands on knees, then bent over at the waist, and finally standing at full height. Even next to the enormous statue, he looked like a giant with his meaty hands, arms, and legs. He easily would have been the biggest man in Sarah's village.

He took off his hat and ran his hands through his thick gray hair. His head seemed particularly large and fleshy, too big for the small hat he had just removed.

Suddenly the branch Sarah was standing on cracked and split and her feet slipped out from under her.

"Ahhh," Sarah gasped, feeling herself falling.

She grabbed onto another branch with both hands and swung in midair for a moment until her feet found a solid branch to rest on.

The watchman quickly turned toward the noise, and she caught a glimpse of an angry red face rimmed by long, bushy gray sideburns and eyebrows. Deep lines creased his forehead, and tiny pink broken blood vessels sprouted on the end of his bulbous nose. But it was his eyes that caught her attention. They were dark and seemed to have a naturally wicked slant. She instinctively shrank back.

Sarah ducked as the watchman hoisted his lantern toward the

noise and squinted into the darkness. He took a step toward the trees, swinging the lantern in front of him, scanning right and left. Sarah held her breath, certain that her red hair would get caught in the lamplight.

Finally, he turned away from her, put the hat back on, and wiped his mouth with the side of his forearm. He checked the time on his pocket watch and then moved off down the path, toward the other side of the island. Lurching right and left, the watchman eventually passed out of sight.

A strong wind blew across the island, making the leaves around Sarah ripple against each other, like a thousand paper fans opening and closing. The wind chilled her and she felt the cold wetness seep into her hair, bones, even the roots of her teeth, making her whole body feel brittle. She had to find a way to get inside and change out of her wet clothes. The only shelter around was the Lady, but she didn't dare venture down yet, not with the gray-haired giant nearby.

And so she waited.

After nearly an hour in the tree, watching and waiting for the giant to return, Sarah climbed down. Her eyes darted back and forth and she kept her body bent low to the ground as she made her way to the path. Her foot kicked against a large shard of broken glass that skidded across the cement with a sharp clang. She stopped in her tracks and listened, afraid that someone would be stirred by the noise. But she heard nothing more.

Sarah looked down at her feet and saw that she had kicked the top of a green glass bottle, and that the other pieces were scattered nearby, including the bottom half of the bottle, which still held a dram of brown liquid. She picked up a piece of glass with the label half stuck on that read GOLDEN CLOVER IRISH WHISKEY and had a picture of a barrel with a clover painted on the side.

Sarah picked up the bottom of the bottle and sniffed the liquid, which was dark, sweet, and medicinal. She began to salivate. It had been hours since her last meal.

Before she could worry about finding food, though, she had to get out of the cold. She set the broken bottle down and hurried toward a door in the Lady's star-shaped base.

The Crown Room

WRAPPING HER HAND AROUND the cold, smooth surface of the brass doorknob, Sarah was certain it would be locked. She jerked her hand back in surprise as the knob yielded in her grasp and the door opened onto a long, dark hallway. Sarah poked her head in and then carefully stepped inside, gasping as the door swung shut.

She fought to regain her breath and adjust to the deep quiet and near-total darkness inside. Sarah blinked her eyes several times, trying to get the space to come into focus, but there was no light to be found. She considered going back outside but couldn't face the idea of returning to the icy chill of the harbor winds. So she felt her way along the hall until she came to the base of a staircase. She started to climb, some inner drive propelling her forward despite her fear.

She came to another hallway and then a door, which opened out onto the star-shaped plaza that formed the roof of the statue's base. Relief swept over her to be back in the moonlight, to be able to see the world around her. She looked up and was again awed by her proximity to the Lady, who drew her ever closer. She needed to be inside the Lady's body, to climb in and around the crown and then up into the torch.

So Sarah forged ahead to the next door at the bottom of the pedestal. She entered the pedestal and again climbed through the darkness until she came out another door, which led directly into the statue itself.

Sarah took another fortifying breath and entered the statue. Once inside, she paused again. The interior space was dark, but not as dark as the base had been. Tiny sprays of moonlight peeked in through small crevices in the statue's shell. Sarah could just make out another long set of winding stairs. Strange, high-pitched whistles of wind blew in and around the interior of the statue above her.

Sarah grabbed the metal railing and started to climb again. After a few dozen steps, she began to sweat despite the cold, and the backs of her legs and ankles started to ache. The stairway wound in tight circles higher and higher. She could tell by the echo that she was inside the skeleton of the statue itself. She imagined the part of the body she might be traveling through, the legs draped in long robes, the waist, the torso, the arm holding the tablet.

Sarah paused to take a breath, her legs and lungs unaccustomed to so much exertion. The tallest building in her village was only two stories high. She flexed her sore legs and kept climbing until she came to a platform in the stairwell. A ladder led off in one direction while the stairs continued up in the other. She took the set of stairs, which narrowed even more. A dim light glowed just ahead.

Finally she came to the top and pulled herself into the observation room inside the crown. The room held a small platform and a set of pyramid-shaped steps that led up to the little windows that formed part of the top of the crown. Sarah climbed the stairs, moved to one of the windows, and peered out. She was winded from the climb, but the view took even more of her breath away. Removing Ivan from her pocket, Sarah placed him up on a window ledge. As Sarah showed Ivan the view, she wished more than anything that her parents could see it too.

She remembered how furious her mother had been when her father came home with the toy. They never had money to spare on anything. As Sarah played with Ivan on her mat, her parents had quietly argued.

"You think we can eat that bear if times get lean?" her mother asked.

"Just look at her!" Sarah's father said, nodding to his daughter. "It was a small price to pay for a little joy."

Her mother watched Sarah playing for a moment, making Ivan jump and roll across her blanket.

"I married a fool," she said. "But a very good-hearted fool."

Now Sarah marveled at the vast amount of land and sea stretched out before her, but also at how small everything looked, like a toy diorama. She could see a bridge connecting the east side of Manhattan with the opposite shore.

She danced Ivan along the ledge of the window, making him tumble and roll as her father used to do to amuse her.

A draft shot through the body of the Lady, chilling Sarah's sweat- and sea-soaked body. She needed to dry herself. So she stood back from the window and started to remove her wet clothes, her boots, coat, stockings, skirt, sweater, and blouse, until she was wearing only her underclothes. She hesitated for a moment, embarrassed to be undressed despite the fact that she was alone. Then she slowly removed her undershirt and underwear until she was completely naked. She wrung out her wet clothes, creating little round puddles on the floor, and draped each article of clothing along the railing of the staircase.

Sarah stood, letting the moonlight bathe her bare skin. Hard goose bumps sprouted across her entire body. Her leg muscles ached from the swim and the climb. She ran her hands over her torso, taking inventory of each muscle, each patch of skin, to confirm that she was still whole, that she was still herself. She paced around the small room, and got used to her own nakedness.

As her hand grazed one of the scrapes on her arm, she felt a horrible pang of loss as she realized her mother would no longer be there to tend her wounds. Yet she also felt glad to be alive.

I am here, she thought. *I'm alive.*

Then all at once exhaustion hit her. She grabbed Ivan off the ledge, laid her coat across a patch of the cold floor just below the windows, and allowed herself to lie down. She exhaled and stared up through the windows in the crown at the clouds drifting across the moon. She listened to the wind blow through the Lady, like the statue itself was breathing.

The noises acted like a lullaby, numbing her mind and making her eyelids heavy. Sarah felt her own breathing slow and relax. Her eyes closed and she fell asleep, naked atop her wet coat.

American Morning

"I'M GONNA BEAT YOU!"

"No, you won't!"

Sarah stirred awake at the echo of voices drifting up from somewhere below and then distant footsteps pounding up a staircase.

"I'm almost there!"

Her eyes shot open, and at first she didn't realize where she was, a strangely shaped gray room with a pyramid staircase and a cold metal floor. A glint of light came through one of the windows at the top of the crown. Suddenly everything came back to her.

She sprang to her feet, her naked body stiff and cold. The joints in her legs, neck, and shoulders cracked as she moved. The voices and footsteps drew nearer.

Sarah grabbed her clothes from the railing. They were still slightly damp and stiff from the night chill, but she pulled them on anyway, racing to cover herself.

The voices came closer.

She struggled to get into her underclothes, skirt, stockings, and blouse. She was just pulling on her sweater as the first tourists came to the foot of the stairs that led to the crown room. A pair of twin boys raced up the final steps. They both had blond hair and wore matching blue coats and knickers.

"I won!" the first boy declared.

But his face fell as he saw the girl awkwardly holding her coat and boots.

"Aw, someone's already up here."

The other twin joined his brother in the observation room.

"How'd you beat us?" he asked. "We were gonna be the first."

Sarah just stared at them, afraid to say anything.

"Maybe she got up here so fast 'cause she took off her shoes," the first twin said.

"Who cares? Look!"

The boys climbed the stairs to the windows and peered out at the view. Sarah quickly pulled on her boots without bothering to lace them, shoved Ivan into her pocket, and hurried for the stairs. As she made her way past dozens of tourists, she kept her head bent low, eyes locked on the steps below her.

Back on the top of the base, she was surrounded by large groups of people waiting in line to enter the statue and milling around staring up at the Lady. She continued down the stairs inside the base until she reached ground level, where hundreds of tourists walked around the island. A ferryboat was moored at the landing dock in the distance, unloading still more passengers.

Her body tensed as she passed directly beside a man wearing an official uniform and hat like the night watchman.

Were they looking for her?

Sarah held her breath. But as he walked past, he didn't seem to notice her at all.

She scanned the island and saw several men in similar uniforms standing at the guard station near the dock and helping tourists with questions and directions. More and more people walked by, none of them taking any notice of a girl all by herself.

No one knows I jumped off the ship, so no one will be looking for me.

Knowing this, Sarah was able to relax a bit and spent the morning walking around the island, trying to blend in with the crowds. Around noon, she followed a young couple. The woman carried a baby wrapped in a pink blanket. The baby's toy rattle fell out of her hand and Sarah instinctively bent to pick it up. The young mother turned to Sarah.

"A sheynem dank," the woman said, thanking her in Yiddish.

Sarah froze, so shocked to hear her native language, she didn't know what to do. Worried about drawing attention to herself in any way, she responded in English, "You're welcome."

She handed the woman the toy and the couple moved on.

Sarah watched them from a distance as they settled on a bench and unpacked a small picnic for themselves. Sarah longed to be with her own mother and father and felt a jolt of envy toward the baby girl. Sarah thought about approaching the family, telling them everything that had happened to her and begging them to help. They seemed so familiar and friendly. She inched closer. But then the mother looked up at her with a curious expression, as if ready to defend her child from anyone coming too close, so Sarah stepped back.

As Sarah walked away, she saw the father cut slices of apple and hand them to the infant. Sarah's mouth filled with saliva at the sight of the food. The father finished slicing and tossed the core into a nearby garbage bin.

Sarah's eyes locked on the bin. She wanted to lunge after the core, but knew she would have to wait until no one was watching. The family ate the apple and then some cheese and crusty bread. The baby girl dropped piles of crumbs as she chomped on an unwieldy corner of the loaf. Sarah was so hungry that even the crumbs looked delicious. Finally, the parents deposited the remnants of their snack in the trash.

As soon as they were a good distance away, Sarah walked toward the trash can, already imagining the taste of the food in her mouth. Just as she was about to reach out her hand, she heard a voice from behind.

"'Scuse me, missy."

An old, brown-skinned man with a round, bald head stood right beside her wearing blue coveralls and pushing a large metal trash can on wheels. The girl joined the flow of people as if she belonged to another family. Her stomach clenched with hunger as she glanced over her shoulder and saw the old man grabbing the garbage bin and emptying it into the can.

She searched the island and found two more trash bins near the door to the entrance of the pedestal, and she nonchalantly positioned herself near one of them to wait for another deposit. Sure enough, a few minutes later a man walked up eating something from a bag, then crumpled it up and threw it away. Sarah wasn't sure what it was, but she knew it was food and hoped that there was some left.

She quickly plunged her hand into the trash can and snatched the bag out, trying to look as if it had been hers all along. Inside she discovered a small pile of white puffs with a warm, savory smell. The outside of the bag was printed in red, white, and blue letters that said "popcorn." She tentatively popped one of the puffs into her mouth and she was surprised how quickly it dissolved on her tongue. She took another handful and the salty treasure made her mouth come alive. As soon as the bag was empty, she craved more.

She spent the morning milling around the trash barrels and managed to scrounge up two half-eaten hot dogs, a piece of a roll with butter, and one bruised banana. She was shocked at how much food was thrown out. In her village, nothing ever went to waste and the idea of throwing away anything even remotely edible was unheard of. Even spoiled food was saved for the goats and other livestock.

Sarah spent the day roaming the island, blending in with the crowds that came and went. As the day progressed, she scavenged more popcorn, a chicken leg, and another half-eaten roll, which she tucked away inside the pocket of her skirt.

Eventually, the crowd thinned and the sun began to set. Sarah became more anxious as there were fewer and fewer people to help camouflage her. One of the men in uniform walked around the island ringing a large brass bell, calling out, "Last boat! All aboard!"

All the tourists made their way down from the Lady and toward the loading dock where the ferry was moored. She followed the crowd toward the boat and stood with the line of people waiting to board.

Sarah knew this was the only way to get to the shores of New York. And she worried about trying to hide alone on the island for another night.

Maybe I can just blend in and get on the boat, she thought.

She stepped into place at the end of the line.

"Tickets! Everyone have your tickets out," the ferryman called from the entrance to the boat.

Each of the passengers handed a ticket to the ferryman as they stepped onto the gangplank. Sarah froze. With no ticket and no money, there was no way for her to sneak past him.

She was trapped on the island.

Cat and Mouse

SARAH SLUNK BACK THROUGH the crowd and made her way toward the Lady, hoping to sneak back inside. But when she got up onto the base's roof, she saw one of the guards standing by the entry door, making sure everyone exited. He called into the doorway.

"Park is closing! Last boat!"

Sarah's eyes darted around, looking for somewhere she could hide.

She ducked back down the stairwell. Maybe there was some sort of storeroom or even a closet. But there were none. Emerging back onto the ground level, she saw the final tourists making their way toward the dock. The guard who had been checking the entry door of the statue was behind her, so she couldn't go back up.

A cold breeze blew off the water and rustled through the leaves. The leaves! She had almost forgotten her hiding spot from the night before. She quickly and carefully maneuvered over to the small patch of trees behind the statue's base. Glancing around to make sure no one was looking, she jumped and grabbed the lowest branch, hauling herself up.

She climbed high into an area with dense cover and settled herself onto a branch to look out. No one had seen her. Peering through the leaves, she could just make out the ferry dock. She saw two of the guards searching the grounds, calling, "All aboard!"

When the last tourists and guards had boarded, the ferry pushed off into the harbor, the fiery sunset bathing everything in a deep orange glow. Sarah exhaled and relaxed onto the branch as the boat steamed north toward Manhattan. She was alone again.

As the sky darkened, Sarah ate some of the food she had been saving, the chicken leg and the half-eaten roll. Soon, though, the wind picked up and the air grew cold and Sarah knew she needed to seek shelter inside. The minutes slowly ticked by and the sun sank lower and lower until the stars appeared above her.

Sarah's skin had chilled and her muscles had tightened by the time she finally ventured down. She ran toward the entrance of the base, but her stiff legs moved awkwardly. Her foot snagged on the corner of one of the large garbage bins along the path and she tripped, falling to her knees. *Clang!* The trash bin tipped over. She paused and listened from the ground.

"Who's there?" a deep, gruff voice called.

Glancing up, Sarah could just make out the figure of the

gray-haired giant emerging from the guardhouse near the ferry dock, holding out his kerosene lamp in the dark.

"I said who is that?" the giant yelled again.

Sarah jumped to her feet and ducked into the shadow of the statue's base.

"Stop!"

He had seen her. Sarah's heart beat faster as she saw him quickly heading up the path toward the statue. She dashed around the building, veering in and around the sharp edges of the enormous base, peeking around the corner each time to see if the man was trailing her.

"Hold it!" he yelled.

But Sarah moved much faster than he did.

"I said stop!"

Finally, she had circled the entire building and was back where she'd started, not too far from the row of the trees in the back. She paused to catch her breath.

I can't just keep running in circles all night, she thought.

She couldn't risk looking for another place to hide on the other side of the island, so she dashed back to her tree and pulled herself up. She had just settled onto a branch with good, leafy cover when she saw the watchman emerge from around the corner of the base.

He held his kerosene lamp in front of him but could barely catch his breath from the effort of the chase. He stopped a few dozen yards from her tree, then put the lamp down and rested his hands on his knees until he could speak again.

"Where are you?" he called into the night.

Sarah held her breath in the silence.

"I know someone's out there."

He stood and listened. A strong wind whipped across the island, causing a loud flutter of leaves all around her.

After the wind died down, he listened for a moment longer and then slowly shambled up toward the entrance to the base.

As the watchman disappeared inside, Sarah exhaled but didn't move. A few moments later, he reemerged on the roof, making his way toward the entrance to the pedestal. Was he going to climb up to the top? Or was there some sort of guardhouse inside the statue?

She heard the sound of his heavy footsteps as he methodically climbed the metal staircase. Aside from the wind and the gentle sound of the waves lapping against the shore, the footsteps were the only sound on the island. *Clank, clomp, clank, clomp, clank, clomp.*

Finally the footsteps stopped and Sarah saw the watchman appear on the Lady's torch. He removed a small bottle from inside his coat and took a long swig. Sarah watched in silence as he stood staring out to sea, taking sips from the bottle and occasionally coughing. Eventually, he screwed the cap back on the bottle and returned it to the pocket inside his jacket, swaying as he made his way along the railing back toward the door to the torch. Suddenly, he lost his footing and the girl gasped, thinking he might go tumbling over the side. But he caught himself on the railing and maneuvered himself back through the door.

The watchman emerged on ground level and stumbled a bit as he walked down toward the guardhouse by the ferry dock. He stopped to take another sip of the whiskey and emptied the bottle into his mouth.

Sarah tensed as he abruptly changed direction and walked toward her tree.

He moved closer and closer, his angry red face seeming to stare straight at her.

This is it, she thought. *He's got me.*

Hunting for Pennies

SARAH LISTENED TO THE sound of the guard's breath wheezing in and out of his mouth as he walked directly beneath her branch. She tried to hold herself as still as possible, tensing every muscle, not allowing herself to take a breath for fear she would make a telltale sound. Despite the cold, sweat sprouted on her forehead as the watchman circled around the tree, scanning the grounds.

Finally he paused and leaned a hand against the tree. Was he going to climb up after her? Sarah closed her eyes tightly. The watchman let out a great belch. Her eyes popped open and she looked down. The giant was leaning over, spitting onto the ground.

Then he straightened his hat and stumbled away.

Sarah watched him walk back to the guardhouse by the dock. Once he was inside, she lowered herself out of the tree. Her joints cracked as she sprinted toward the base and slipped in through the door. She paused to catch her breath, took off her boots so her bare feet would not make any noise on the steps, and then climbed up and into the statue as quickly as she could. She made it all the way to the crown room and settled herself down for the night.

Relief swept over Sarah. The oddly shaped crown felt familiar and cozy, and she was already starting to think of it as *her* room. She climbed the small set of stairs that led to the windows and looked out at the harbor. Had any girl ever had a more spectacular view from her bedroom?

She had found part of an old torn kerchief, which she used to make a tiny bed for Ivan that she placed right beside her. Then she covered herself with a brown shawl she had discovered abandoned on a bench earlier that day and tucked her arm under her head for a pillow. She imagined costumed servants running up and down the stairs to serve them platters of fruit and cheese as if she were a princess in the tower of a castle.

As she stared up at the stars through the windows of the crown, Sarah's relief turned to worry. Sarah knew she had to get off the island before she got caught. Earlier in the day, she had found a penny on the ground behind one of the benches. Maybe she could collect enough to buy her passage to Manhattan.

The next morning, she was more prepared for the arrival of the tourists. As the first ferry arrived, she watched from her window and then came down and sneaked up the ladder to the torch, thinking that most early climbers would want to go to the crown first. As soon as the first group walked up, she emerged from the torch and walked down to the pedestal.

She wandered down to the boat launch and saw a sign on the

boat that read: FERRY TICKETS 25 CENTS. She looked at her penny. One cent. She only needed twenty-four more. The question was, could she evade the watchman for long enough to find them?

Sarah spent the next few days on the island wandering around and trying to blend in with the tourists. She scavenged food and drinks from the garbage when no one was looking and managed to find a few more pennies in places where people sat or gathered.

Every day tourists discarded newspapers, so Sarah had plenty to read in both English and Yiddish. Occasionally she'd find a paper in a completely foreign language, and she made a game of trying to figure out what the stories were about based on the pictures.

At night, she hid in her tree until the watchman had made his rounds. Every evening, he followed the same routine of climbing up to the torch, staring out to sea, and drinking from his bottle. And each night he'd come down and toss the empty bottle into the bay. To Sarah it felt like a game of cat and mouse, with her scurrying in and around the statue to avoid him.

As she lay with Ivan in the crown room at night, she'd carefully count out her pennies, first three, then seven, then fifteen.

"Only ten more," she said to Ivan. "Then we can get to the promised land." Being so close to her goal made Sarah miss her mother even more. She imagined how proud Mama would be if Sarah made it to New York on her own.

Threat of Rain

ON HER FIFTH DAY ON THE ISLAND, Sarah woke to a strange pinging sound in the crown room. The sky was gray and a light rain was falling. Anxiety gripped her. Would any tourists come? If not, where would she hide? How would she eat?

Luckily, even in the rain, people visited the island—not as many, but still enough to provide cover. Sarah found an abandoned umbrella that someone had left on a bench and was able to lose herself in the crowd. Scavenging for food proved to be more difficult as no one was picnicking. The entire day went by without her finding a scrap of food or a single penny.

Even so, Sarah was grateful when the last boat was boarded and she could hide in her tree. The moist branches were slippery, and she had to move carefully so that her hands and feet wouldn't slide off the bark as she shimmied her way up.

The rain fell harder as the night watchman emerged from the guardhouse and made his way up to the statue. He moved more slowly than usual and swayed and halted a bit, as if he had already started drinking before his shift. Sarah wondered if he would walk out on the torch's platform even on such a miserable night. She hoped he'd skip that part of his ritual so that she could return to her nest in the crown room. But sure enough, he climbed up the Lady and emerged onto the torch just as he had every other night.

As the cold rain soaked her to the skin, the minutes felt like hours. She wished he would hurry up and finish his ritual so she could get out of the cold. Yet he seemed to stay out there even longer than usual, sipping from his bottle and staring into the rainy darkness.

At last, he turned and made his way back inside. *Thank goodness.* Sarah was soaked to the bone. She also had to go to the bathroom. She waited impatiently for the gray-haired giant to reappear, but he didn't. Ten minutes passed, then twenty, then forty, then an hour, until her gut ached with the effort to hold it in. Finally she couldn't wait anymore.

She lowered herself from the tree, ducked behind the trunk, and lifted her skirt. Warm relief spread through her body. But as soon as she was finished, the cold overtook her again. The rain fell still harder, and Sarah wondered if the watchman was waiting out the storm inside the statue.

She sat herself under the tree and continued to wait. Another hour passed and the rain tapered off and stopped, but still the watchman didn't appear. Could he have already left the statue? How could she have missed that?

The temperature dropped even more, and Sarah felt frost forming on the outside of her clothes, stiffening her hair like frozen blades of grass on a winter morning. An icy rain began to fall again, this time even harder than before. She had to get inside.

Maryk

RAIN AND WIND THRASHED the Lady as Sarah slowly climbed up the stairs in the darkness. She paused every few steps to listen for any sign of the watchman, but every time she did, she heard only the pinging of the rain and the shrill whistle of the wind rushing in and around the statue's metal skin.

She rose higher and higher until she came to the landing that led to the ladder up to the torch. Sarah paused to catch her breath before continuing to her makeshift bedroom.

She had taken one step into the darkness toward the stairs when her foot struck something soft and solid.

"Ugh."

She jumped back.

The giant!

Every impulse in her body told her to turn around and run back down the stairs. But then she heard a soft moan. She tentatively extended her foot once more. When her foot touched him, he groaned again, and she quickly pulled it back.

She knelt down beside his body and ran her hand slowly along the ground until it hit something warm and sticky. She shuddered fora moment at the memory of her father's blood on the night he died. She reached out her hand and found the watchman's arm. He didn't react, so she boldly ran her hand up his arm to his face. Halfway up his forehead, a deep gash was forming along the hairline. Suddenly his hand shot up out of the darkness and grabbed her wrist tightly. She tried to pull her arm back, but he held her firm.

"Help," he rasped.

Finally he released her. Adrenaline roared through her body as she grasped the guardrail and pulled herself down the staircase. She was halfway back down when she stopped and listened. Silence. He wasn't following her. She stood in the darkness a long moment, weighing the risks, as she listened to her own breathing and thought of the man's labored gasps.

What if he dies up there and I could have done something to save him?

She felt Ivan in her pocket and recalled a memory of her father.

He had been walking her to a friend's birthday party when they came upon a man on the village road whose cart had overturned. Her father stopped to help him. Sarah had grown frustrated because she knew they would be late for the party.

"But we don't even know this man, Papa," she whispered. "Can't we let him wait for someone he knows to help him? Surely someone will come along."

"If everyone thought that way, he might be waiting forever, Sarah," her father said. "We have an obligation to do God's work.

Even if it makes us late for a party."

Sarah stood another moment and then climbed back up the stairs until she reached the landing. She stood above the groaning watchman's body, trying to figure out what to do. He rolled over and Sarah took a quick step back. He slowly raised his arm.

"Help me up," he said.

She grabbed his hands and tugged, trying to hoist him to his feet. He was more than three times her weight, and it took all of her effort to help him regain his footing. When she finally got him to stand up, he swayed and toppled over. Sarah threw herself against his side to prop him up and buckled under his weight, but she managed to keep both of them from falling. Carefully balancing him on his unsteady feet, she threw her arm around his back and rested some of his bulk on her shoulder. She knew that she could never make it all the way back down with him. Her only option was to try to get him up the final set of stairs to the crown room, where at least there would be some small amount of light.

Sarah maneuvered the giant to the stairs, placed his hands on the railing, and pushed him from behind. Ever so slowly, she shoved him up, pausing every few steps so they could catch their breath and steady themselves. By the time they reached the top, they were both panting and sweaty.

The giant emerged into the crown room first and immediately collapsed onto all fours, struggling to catch his breath. He rolled over onto his back. His eyes flickered shut and his head rolled to the side.

Because of the rain, the room was much darker than usual, but some moonlight was breaking through the clouds, and in the faint light she was able to make out more of his face: his thick gray hair, his large nose, his strange eyes, and the deep gash that ran along the side of his head. A silver badge glinted on his chest. It read MARYK.

Sarah's mother had taught her some basic first aid. She took her gray scarf and bound it tightly around the man's head to stanch the flow of blood. As she folded her coat into a pillow and placed it behind his head, she could smell the whiskey and tobacco on his breath.

Once she had him settled, she sat against the back wall to catch her breath. She heard the rain slowly subside and stop. She needed a place to think about what to do next, away from the giant, so she retreated from the crown room and climbed up into the torch.

She had never been on the torch at night. As she came out onto the platform, a huge gust of wind blew back her hair and made her grab the railing. Once she had steadied herself, a thrill ran through her body. The thick clouds had parted just enough for her to see a yellow half-moon in the far distance, casting the whole sky in dramatic purple shadows. It felt dangerous to be in the open air at such a great height in the dark. Sarah finally understood why the watchman might have been coming up here every night.

But what would she do now? Should she leave and hope some-one would find him in the morning? Where would she hide for the night? Her only choice was to stay with him and hope that he'd sleep long enough to give her time to sneak out in the morning the way she normally did.

Sarah took one last deep breath of night air and then went inside and climbed to the crown room, where she found Maryk snoring just where she'd left him. She sat herself in a corner with her back against the wall and her knees pulled to her chest and waited.

Roast Beef and a Pickle

SARAH COULD FEEL THE sun warming her face and brightening her closed eyelids. Still half asleep, she heard the muted *clang* of footsteps in the distance.

The tourists!

Her eyes shot open, and she recoiled at the sight of Maryk's prone body sleeping in the center of the room. In the light of the cramped crown room, he seemed even larger than he had before. She couldn't believe that she had been able to get him up the stairs the night before. He shifted in his sleep, snoring. The voices of the tourists grew nearer.

Sarah jumped to her feet, gathered her few articles of clothing, and dashed out of the room. Running down the top section of stairs, she reached the platform that led to the ladder up to the torch just before the first few visitors passed by on their way to the crown.

Seconds later she heard a woman scream and then a man say, "My God! What's happened here?"

"Someone get help!" another voice chimed in.

Sounds of people scurrying up and down the stairs and talking about the unconscious watchman filled the Lady's interior. There was so much commotion that no one noticed the girl descending the torch ladder.

Sarah exited onto ground level just as two guards ran up to tend to the injured man. She backed away slowly and hid herself among a group of tourists to watch. Eventually another group of men ran up from the dock carrying a stretcher. A half hour later the men came down from the statue, struggling under the weight of the giant. The watchman appeared to be conscious but in a great deal of pain. It took four men to carry him down to the dock, one holding each arm of the stretcher. The giant winced and grunted with each step they took.

Sarah ducked behind a crowd of gawkers, not wanting to be seen. She wondered if the giant would be able to recognize her or if he even remembered anything from the night at all. *Do drunk people remember things?* The four men carefully loaded him onto a ferry that steamed off toward Manhattan. She exhaled with relief. At least for now, her biggest threat of being caught would be off the island.

Over the next two days, Sarah was able to return to her routine of scavenging by day and sneaking into the Lady to sleep at night. A new night watchman took over. Short, with thick glasses, he had a pinched scowl that made him look constantly angry. Unlike the gray-haired giant, the new watchman didn't drink or climb to the top of the torch and stare out to sea. He simply walked the grounds once with his kerosene lamp and then returned to the guardhouse by the dock.

Sarah wondered about the giant. Had he died? And if not, when would he recover and come back? Whatever his fate, she hoped he wouldn't return to work soon; her life was much easier with the new watchman. She could enter the Lady as soon as the sun went down and not have to be worried about being disturbed during the night.

On the afternoon of the third day since the giant's accident, Sarah retrieved a paper sack containing a large piece of roast beef, some potato salad, and a pickle from one of the trash bins. Compared to the scraps of snack food like peanuts and popcorn that she had been eating, it was a feast. Later, she scavenged a half-full jar of lemonade. All afternoon she dreamed of the wonderful meal she would have that night in the crown room.

Part of her routine was to climb up to the roof of the pedestal and scan the island to see if anyone was throwing away anything down below. Although she had already scavenged more than usual that day, her heart rose up as she spied a man standing near the dock carelessly throwing a half-eaten apple into a trash bin.

The perfect dessert for her feast.

She dashed off down the stairs of the base, hoping to get to her prize before the trash bin was emptied. Reaching ground level, she wove through the tourists toward the dock. The trash bin came into view and she could see the apple perched right on top, ready for the picking.

Sarah was just a few yards away when she accidentally bumped into someone coming up from the dock. She looked up and to her horror stared into the face of the giant. His strange eyes stared down at her.

Mouse Trap

THE GIANT HAD A LARGE BANDAGE wrapped around his head, and two of the fingers on his left hand were taped together.

Sarah froze. Did he recognize her?

"Watch where you're goin'," he grunted.

"I am sorry," she mumbled.

He paused a moment and stared at her impatiently but then moved past.

Sarah immediately turned from the trash bin and walked in a different direction, breathing a sigh of relief. She spent the rest of the afternoon staying as far away from the watchman as possible. When the sun finally went down, she retreated to her tree to wait and watch.

As usual, the giant emerged from the guardhouse and slowly moved toward the statue. He didn't appear to sway or wobble, and Sarah assumed that he had not been drinking.

Just like every other night, he entered the statue and climbed up to the torch to stare out to sea. Yet this time, he didn't drink from a bottle of Irish whiskey or anything else. He just stood and stared, breathing in the ocean air. After a little while, he turned and scanned the whole island, and the girl instinctively drew back into the leaves. Finally, the watchman went back inside, descended the Lady, and returned to the guardhouse.

Sarah's stomach growled, yet she waited another long stretch, staring at the dim yellow light that glowed from inside the guardhouse by the ferry dock just to make sure he had settled in for the night. Finally she lowered herself down from the tree and sneaked inside the statue.

Once in the crown room, Sarah spread out her shawl and unpacked her feast. The moon glowed brightly, and she could clearly see each item: the pickle, potato salad, roast beef, and lemonade. She set Ivan beside the food.

"This is a meal fit for a queen," she said. "Isn't it, boy?"

She reached for the pickle and took an enormous bite, savoring the sour, briny crunch. She pretended to give Ivan some too and smiled to herself as she took another big bite. Suddenly she heard a loud creak.

She held her jaw still, afraid the crunch of the pickle would keep her from hearing more. Silence. She waited a moment longer, then resumed chewing. But as she swallowed, she heard another creak from deep within the body of the Lady and then the unmistakable sound of footsteps, rising up the stairs.

The giant was coming.

Sarah shoved Ivan back into her pocket, rolled up her picnic dinner in the shawl, and stuffed it into a corner of the room. But where would she hide herself? She glanced down into the stairwell and saw a dim light approaching from below. *Clang, clomp, clang, clomp, clang, clomp.*

Her only choice was to hide herself right there in the crown room. Quickly, Sarah unrolled the picnic and covered herself in the shawl, curling into a tight ball in the most shadowy corner of the room, beneath the windows of the crown. She sat under the thick fabric and tried to control her breathing as the footsteps drew closer up the winding staircase. Sitting directly on top of the remnants of her feast, she tried to ignore the strong aroma of the roast beef.

Through the fabric, Sarah saw the room brighten as the watchman's lamp entered the crown. She clamped her eyes shut and held her breath, trying to hold herself as still as possible. Sweat formed on her forehead and dripped down her face, causing her nose and eyes to itch. Breathing heavily, the giant stepped inside and swung his lamp around the room. Sarah counted his long, wheezing breaths.

One, two, three, four, five . . .

She felt a sneeze rising up inside her and clenched all of her face muscles to suppress it. The giant finally turned and moved to exit. Just as he reached the stairs, he coughed. The noise startled Sarah and triggered her own sneeze. She clamped her fingers over her nose to stifle the noise, but a small, high-pitched squeak came out of the back of her throat.

The giant paused. Sarah opened her eyes and saw the fabric over her face brightening as he moved nearer, stopping directly in front of her. He stood over her a moment and then pulled off the shawl, leaving her exposed in the kerosene light. He swung the lamp in her direction and the yellow light flashed brightly in her eyes.

"Who are you?" he demanded.

Sarah blinked to clear her vision and looked up into the giant's broad, angry face. His ruddy complexion starkly contrasted with his gray helmet of hair. A small patch of dried blood stained the front of the white bandage. He glared and she drew back as though she could somehow hide from him.

"I said, who are you? And what are you doing here?"

Sarah was so frozen by fear that she couldn't respond.

"Why are you up here?"

She stared back silently.

"Stand up and come over here!" he said. "Are you deaf or something?"

Still she didn't budge.

"Can you hear me?"

Her mind had cleared enough for her to nod. *Yes.*

"Can you speak?"

She nodded again.

"Well, who are you?"

Sarah was afraid to answer, certain that as soon as her identity was revealed, she'd be put back on a boat bound for her country and her dreaded uncle or an orphanage. She decided to pretend she didn't understand his language to buy herself time.

"English, just a little," she said.

The giant gruffly motioned for her to come out from the corner.

"Come on."

She reluctantly uncurled herself. As she stood, the roast beef and pickle dropped onto the floor from the back of her skirt. He took in the food with surprise.

"What the . . . ? Do people always sit on their meals in your country?"

He kicked at the precious roast beef with his boot and she looked down at her feet in shame. Her eyes welled up. She was sure that he would know she was a thief and that she would be in even more trouble. She cursed herself for not having shoved the food into her mouth at the first sign of danger.

"Hungry," she said. "I . . . am hungry."

He stared down at the piece of roast beef and the pickle, which were now covered in a layer of dust.

"Come on," he said. "Get out of there. Let's go."

He gestured for her to move to the stairs. She hesitated and looked at the food.

"Leave it," he said.

She remained frozen, so he reached out and poked her shoulder to prod her along.

"I said leave it. Now go on."

Sarah's hands shook as she grabbed the railing to begin her descent.

Androcles

SARAH SLOWLY STARTED DOWN the stairs, the giant close behind her. She calculated her escape options. Once they were back on ground level, she hesitated.

Should I run?

She knew that if she made a break for the trees, he'd just catch her again. And she couldn't face the idea of diving into the freezing water.

The giant coughed violently and paused to catch his breath. Sarah knew this was her opportunity to run, but her legs locked beneath her. After a moment, he prodded her.

"Okay, let's go," he said. "Move."

He steered her toward the guardhouse. The wind whipped off the water and into Sarah's face. Wild thoughts ran through her mind.

There's no one around until morning. What will he do with me? Will he beat me? Lock me up?

Once at the guardhouse she stopped at the door.

"Go on," he said. "Inside."

The giant opened the door to the small shack. Sarah hesitated again. He poked her in the back with his finger.

"I said go on."

Sarah took a deep breath and stepped inside. The sparsely furnished room held a desk, a low wooden cabinet, and a couple of chairs. Posters with the ferry schedule and maps of the harbor lined the walls.

"Sit," he said, gesturing to one of the chairs.

She did as instructed and bent her head.

The giant opened one of the cabinet drawers and rummaged inside. Was he looking for chains to lock her up?

Sarah stared down at the tabletop, afraid to look at his angry face again, until he placed something on the table in front of her. She glanced up and was surprised to see a small tin pot covered with a lid. He continued searching in the drawer until he found a spoon, wiped it on his shirt, and laid it next to the pot.

"Go on," the watchman said, nodding toward the table.

She stared at the pot and spoon, unsure what to do.

"Eat," he commanded.

He lifted the cover. A warm and mysterious smell hit her nose. The pot held a pile of browned rice mixed with a white stew of some kind, with pieces of chicken, celery, onion, cabbage, and some sort of sprouts, all mixed together.

"Well, dig in." He nodded toward the food.

Sarah lifted the spoon and took a small bite. It had been so long since her last cooked meal. And while not hot, the food was warm and it exploded in her mouth with a burst of flavor that made her eyes close with pleasure. Despite her fear, a small smile escaped her lips as the food traveled down her throat and into her empty stomach. The giant nodded.

"Mrs. Lee isn't the best landlady in the world, but she makes a good chop suey."

The giant stuffed and lit a pipe and curiously watched her hungrily devour the entire contents of the pot. When she had scraped up the last grain of rice, she laid the spoon down and looked at the giant.

"Thank you," she said.

He nodded.

"Now, are you going to tell me who you are?"

She stared back at him, unsure of what she should share or not.

"Come on, out with it. I'm not gonna hurt you, Androcles."

"What is Androcles?" she asked.

He raised an eyebrow and slowly restuffed his pipe. "Androcles was a Greek slave. One day he found an injured lion with a thorn in his paw and pulled out the thorn. Years later, Androcles was thrown into the arena with a lion. Turned out to be the same lion, and he remembered Androcles and refused to hurt him. You get it?"

She stared at him, confused.

"Look," he said, "I don't remember much about the other night, but I know you helped me. And I'm not gonna forget that. I want to help you. But you have to tell me who you are and how you got here. Where are your parents?"

"My parents?"

"Yes, your mother and father. Where's your mother?"

She hesitated and then said the word.

"Dead."

"And your father?"

"He's dead too."

"You're an orphan." He raised his eyebrows with interest.

Sarah nodded.

"Hmmm," he grunted.

He took a long drag on his pipe.

"What's your name?"

Sarah just looked at him.

He pointed at his chest and said, "Maryk." Then he pointed at her. "And you are . . . ?"

The girl stared into Maryk's dark eyes, which now seemed softer. It had been more than a week since she had heard or said her own name, and the word felt strange coming out of her mouth.

"Sarah."

The Niece

MARYK SHARED HIS CONTAINER of coffee with Sarah as she told him her story. She had never tasted coffee before, and at first the bitterness shocked her; but soon its warmth spread through her body, helping to thaw her cold fingers and toes.

Maryk sat and listened while smoking his pipe. He didn't ask many questions as she spoke, but nodded, encouraging her to continue.

Days of silence had created a pent-up need for Sarah to talk. So she told him everything, from her life in the village, to the attack that killed her father, to the promise of the Lady and the tantalizing poem on the postcard. She even recited part of the poem from memory.

"'Give me your tired, your poor, / Your huddled masses yearning to breathe free.'"

"Powerful words." He nodded.

Eventually, she described her daring leap from the ship and her swim to shore.

"It's a miracle you survived," Maryk said with a trace of admiration.

"Yes. A miracle," she said.

Next she told Maryk about her days scavenging on the island and her nights playing cat and mouse with him, escaping into the tree to hide and the Lady to sleep.

The sun was just beginning to rise as she finished her story.

"I can't go back to my country. There is nothing for me there but bad thoughts."

"Memories," he corrected.

"Yes. Bad memories. But bad thoughts, too. I mean, things, bad things. People here don't understand. There's danger there for people like me, who are different. Our men cannot be in the army, our people can't own land. Everyone thinks America is a different kind of country."

Maryk nodded.

"I suppose it can be . . . sometimes."

Maryk seemed about to say more, but then a bell rang in the distance and he looked up in alarm.

"Oh no," he muttered as he rose and moved to the window.

Outside in the harbor, a ferry approached. Sarah knew that this was the first boat of the morning, which would bring the day staff to the island and take the night watchman back to the mainland.

Through the window of the guardhouse, Sarah saw three uniformed men disembark from the boat, including the short man with glasses who had been Maryk's replacement on the night shift after the accident. Two of the men walked toward the base of the statue. The man with the glasses came toward the guardhouse. Maryk's face filled with concern. He turned to Sarah and stared at her for a long, tense moment.

What would he do with her now? she wondered. Would he turn her in? And if not, how would he ever explain her being here?

Sarah looked out the window at the nearby trees and the waves lapping against the shore. She again calculated her limited escape options: run and hide in the tree or in the Lady, or dive into the water and attempt to swim away. Both ideas seemed impossible. She was in Maryk's hands.

Maryk also seemed to be considering his options. Then he hastily turned and cleared their coffee cups from the table and straightened the room.

"Just follow my lead and don't say anything, okay?"

"Follow you?"

"Yes. But don't say too much if anyone asks you questions. Just short answers. Do you understand?"

"Yes. I think."

"Short answers," he said. "Yes and no."

Maryk straightened his jacket just as the man with the glasses reached the guardhouse, entered, and then took a step back in surprise. His eyes narrowed in on Sarah and then Maryk, who awkwardly stiffened his posture. There was a tense moment of silence. Sarah sensed that the two men didn't like each other.

She tried not to show her fear, by making her face as

expressionless as possible.

"What have we here?" the man said, arching an eyebrow. "You bring a drinking partner out with you last night, Maryk?"

Sarah could tell by the man's tone that it was not a friendly question.

"No. I didn't have anything to drink last night. Haven't in two days."

"Two days? Is that a record? I guess I wouldn't want to be distracted by booze either if I had my girlfriend with me."

"This is my niece, Johnson. So watch your mouth."

"Your niece?"

"Yes," Maryk said.

"Didn't know they had redheaded Indians. Redskins, yes. Redheads, no. I guess you half-breeds never know what you're gonna look like, do you? You're kind of like mutts that way."

"Watch it."

Maryk took a step toward Johnson, who threw up his hands in mock surrender.

"What's your name, girl?" he said, turning to Sarah.

She stared back dumbly.

"Her name is Sarah," Maryk said.

"Yes. Sarah," she confirmed, nodding quickly.

"Come on, Sarah, let's go."

Maryk took her by the arm to lead her out of the guardhouse.

Johnson stepped in front of them, blocking the door.

"You know there are rules about having guests on the night

shift, don't you?" The man with the glasses looked her up and down. "Even if she is your *niece*."

Sarah could tell by his tone that he doubted their story.

"Let's go," Maryk said.

He pushed Sarah out the door and moved to board the ferry.

"Don't look back," Maryk said. "Just get on the boat."

Sarah followed Maryk's orders and boarded. The ferryboat captain seemed to know Maryk and nodded to him as they settled themselves in the passengers' compartment belowdecks.

Chinatown

"DON'T MIND JOHNSON," MARYK SAID. "He and I don't get along. It has nothing to do with you. He's been angling to get my job for his brother. You understand?"

Sarah didn't really, but she nodded anyway.

She sat beside Maryk on the cold metal bench. They were the only passengers on board. An eerie, high-pitched squeal of wind swept through the boat's interior, amplifying the silence between them. It was strange sitting next to Maryk in the semidarkness. For so long, he had been a scary giant whom she had avoided at all costs. Now, she was willingly following him even though she had no idea where he would take her. A chill settled over her as she recalled her mother warning her about strangers. She glanced at Maryk out of the corner of her eye, afraid to turn to look at him directly.

He seemed to be lost in his own thoughts, but his expression was hard and inscrutable. He closed his eyes and leaned his head against the back wall of the ferry. Then she noticed that both of his hands shook as he tried to hold them steady on his knees.

Sarah gazed out the window at the Lady, whose strong, beautiful face seemed to be staring right at her. She was anxious about leaving the familiarity of the island, but also felt a rush of excitement at the prospect of finally reaching the shores of New York.

When the ferry pulled into the dock, Maryk abruptly stood.

"Come on." He took her by the arm and led her up to the top deck and then down the gangplank.

Sarah paused before stepping onshore. What would it feel like to finally set foot on the promised land?

"Let's go," Maryk said impatiently.

He pulled her along onto the street. Although the ground beneath her feet felt no different, her eyes, ears, and nose were overwhelmed by everything around her. She marveled at the sheer number of buildings lined up along the twisting streets and avenues, pressed together so close that they touched. Sarah was instantly jostled by a man in a bowler hat rushing along, reading his newspaper. The man didn't even pause to say "excuse me"; he just kept walking.

Horse-drawn carriages clattered down the avenue so loudly that she had to block her ears. Pushcart vendors called out their wares and newsboys shouted headlines trying to get people to buy their papers.

Sarah was surprised at the number of newsboys and the variety of papers in different languages being sold. She tried to read the bold stories on the front pages, but she and Maryk were moving too fast for her to digest the words.

A familiar smell struck her nose and she just managed to step around a fresh pile of horse manure. The cobblestone streets were covered with enough to fertilize all the farms back home. Dozens of horses trotted by on the street. Sarah jumped back, positioning herself close to the buildings, as far away from the animals as possible.

As they came to a corner, a horse-drawn milk cart cut in front of them. Sarah recoiled.

"What's the matter?" Maryk said.

"The horses . . ."

"What about them?"

"There are so many."

"So?"

"I . . . don't like them."

"Can't be scared of horses if you expect to walk down the streets of Manhattan," he said. "Now, let's go."

He pulled her impatiently by the arm and they continued their trek.

As they walked east, a massive stone tower appeared in the distance, topped with an American flag. Sarah gasped at the sight of it, thinking it must be the top of a huge castle or military fortress. Moving closer, she saw that there were actually two massive towers connected by a web of steel cables and that the whole thing was actually a bridge stretching over a wide river. As the full bridge came into view, she stopped in her tracks to admire it.

Sarah had seen the bridge from the island but hadn't understood how big it really was. It made the statue of the Lady seem small by comparison. Sarah's eyes widened as she noticed the scores of people and wagons crossing back and forth.

"What's the matter?" Maryk said. "It's just the Brooklyn Bridge."

"How does the road not fall into the water with all the horses and wagons riding on it?"

"Do I look like an engineer? Come on. We're not too far now."

They continued walking uptown, passing City Hall and other large and impressive stone buildings.

Eventually they came to a series of streets that were more densely crowded with pedestrians and pushcarts. Nearly every person they passed had black hair, narrow eyes, and light beige skin. Many were dressed in strange clothes: men in plain blue, black, or gray tunics with ties instead of buttons, and a small handful of women in robes and plain dresses in the same colors. Some of the men wore their hair in long braids. They all seemed to be speaking a language that wasn't English. Sarah stopped in her tracks, afraid to continue. Maryk turned to her, exasperated.

"What is it now?"

"This is still the United States?" Sarah asked.

"Yes."

"But the people . . . are they Americans?"

"Most of them are Chinese. You've heard of China, haven't you?"

"Yes," she said.

"Can't be afraid of horses or Chinamen if you expect to live in New York," he said impatiently.

He continued walking as she tentatively followed. She noticed that all the store signs were written in strange, unfamiliar letters, set against bold-colored backgrounds. Newsboys sold papers printed in the same alien characters. Pushcart vendors peddled exotic fruits and colorful trinkets. Some even had small coal stoves where men prepared food cooked in hot oil.

Sarah breathed deeply to catch the enticing aroma of the food, but almost as soon as she'd managed to capture a good smell, her nose would be assaulted by an equally powerful stench as they passed a pile of garbage or an open fish market where an old man cleaned and gutted the daily catch on the curb. They walked by butcher shops whose windows were festooned with whole plucked ducks and geese and enormous pig carcasses alongside cages tightly packed with live chickens. Sarah couldn't believe the sharp contrast in the sights, smells, and people she had encountered in the course of a few blocks.

Maryk turned onto a narrow side street and stopped in front of a squat, gray six-floor apartment building that seemed to sag in the middle. A steep set of cracked concrete stairs led up to the entry door with a wooden sign attached to the outside wall by the front window. The sign had large Chinese characters painted against a black backdrop along with small English letters at the bottom reading ROOMS TO LET.

Maryk ascended the stairs, beckoning Sarah to follow.

Again the girl paused, her inner warning bells telling her that this might be her last opportunity to escape from Maryk.

Before she had time to consider which way she should run, the front door of the apartment building swung open and a tiny old Chinese woman emerged, yelling at Maryk in a high-pitched, rapid-fire mix of Chinese and broken English. The woman had a small, angry face and shiny gray hair pulled back in a tight bun, and her skinny frame was draped in a black housedress and a long blue knitted coat. The sight of her fearlessly scolding Maryk, who was nearly three times her size, was so funny, Sarah had to bite her bottom lip to keep herself from laughing.

Mrs. Lee

"WHY YOU LEAVE LAUNDRY bag on stairs? Mrs. Lee almost break her neck! You want that? You want to kill old Chinese lady?"

"No," Maryk managed to reply.

"I tell you to leave laundry in hallway next to back door. What you not understand about that? I speak English perfect."

"I know. I forgot."

"You forget? You forget and Mrs. Lee end up dead at the bottom of stairs." She wagged her finger in his face. "Then who do your laundry? Who cook your meals?"

"Sorry."

"No. Sorry won't do laundry. Mrs. Lee do laundry. Mrs. Lee cook meals. But Mrs. Lee can't do that if she dead at the bottom of the stairs because you left your smelly bag of clothes for me to trip on."

Sarah let out a small giggle. It was the first time she had laughed in weeks. Mrs. Lee paused in her rant and turned to the girl.

"Who are you?" she asked.

"It's a long story," said Maryk.

"Long story? I just ask who she is. Why that a long story?"

Sarah froze, wondering if Maryk would attempt to continue the illusion that she was his niece. Before he had time to say anything, Mrs. Lee yelled again.

"I run a clean house, Maryk. I don't let painted ladies in my house."

"She's not a painted lady."

"No, she too skinny for that," Mrs. Lee said, appraising Sarah's frame.

Sarah straightened her posture.

"Who is she, then?"

"Like I said, it's a long story."

"I don't want girl with long story in my house."

Maryk paused and exhaled a deep breath.

"She's in trouble," he said. "And she needs help."

Mrs. Lee crossed her arms, and her eyes narrowed on Sarah.

"You speak?"

"Yes," Sarah replied.

"What kind of trouble you in?"

"Look, can we go inside?" Maryk said. "I can explain."

Mrs. Lee looked hard at Sarah and then Maryk.

"Five minutes inside. But then out! I don't want trouble."

Sarah and Maryk followed Mrs. Lee inside. The interior hall-way was dark with faded pink-and-blue floral wallpaper and a simple rag rug on the floor. A gaslight fixture hung from the ceiling, letting out shafts of yellow light and making a low hiss. Mrs. Lee led them to the front room just off the hall, and they all sat around a large wooden table that occupied most of the first-floor parlor.

Maryk sat beside Sarah as she retold her story. By the time Sarah had finished, an hour had passed. Mrs. Lee sat with her arms crossed and eyes narrowed as she looked up at Maryk. She hadn't said a word the entire time.

"What you planning to do with her?"

"I don't know," he said. "But for now, I thought she could stay here and help you run the house."

"I have Smitty and Miss Jean to run house," Mrs. Lee shot back.

"She could help with the cooking," Maryk offered.

"You think I need help to cook?"

"No. But . . ."

"I can do any work," Sarah said. "I'll work very hard."

"What if people ask questions?" Mrs. Lee said, turning to Maryk. "Don't want anyone think I force the girl to work or do something illegal."

"They won't," Maryk said.

"So some strange girl just appear at my door . . ."

"Please," Sarah interrupted. "I won't make any trouble. And I will work hard. I promise."

"The kid could use a break," Maryk said.

Mrs. Lee took in the girl and exhaled.

"You can stay one week. One week only. But after that, you have to go. Understand?"

"Yes," Sarah said.

She had no idea what she would do after that, but it was better than nothing.

"It's dangerous for Mrs. Lee to have you here, so you make no trouble." She turned to Maryk. "She sleep in your room, you sleep in basement. No funny business."

"Of course," Maryk said.

"Mrs. Lee have a soft heart and stupid head," she said.

"Thank you," Sarah said.

She pointed to Maryk. "You go set up cot in basement." Then she turned to Sarah. "You come with me."

Mrs. Lee led her to the kitchen at the back of the first floor. Tall white cabinets lined one wall, and a large stove and icebox stood against the other. A deep old porcelain bathtub sat beside a galvanized metal sink and faucet.

"Take off clothes," she said.

"Excuse me?" Sarah said.

"You stink like old fish. Need a bath."

Mrs. Lee filled a battered brass teakettle and several pots and set them to boil on the stove. She filled the tub with some cold water from the tap and then mixed in the hot water as it came to a boil.

Sarah had never been naked in front of anyone but her mother. The last thing she wanted to do was to undress in front of this strange woman.

Stripped and Scrubbed

"No one take bath with clothes on," Mrs. Lee said. "And I can't have stinky fish girl in house. Go on, before water get cold."

Sarah slowly started to undress. Mrs. Lee bustled about and continued to talk.

"I see lots of naked girls before. I have two daughters. Grown now. And I'm a girl too. Old, but still a girl. I've got same parts as you."

Sarah had not disrobed completely since the first night she'd swum ashore, and she felt her entire body lighten as she unpeeled layer after layer. Dirt and grime were caked on most of her body, along with several cuts and bruises from her various falls and bumps. Mrs. Lee noticed her ravaged skin and shook her head.

"You all skin and bones. Dirty skin and bones. Get in."

Sarah carefully dipped a toe into the water, and the warmth traveled up her leg and into her entire body. She stepped in and submerged herself. Every pore seemed to breathe a sigh of relief upon contact with the warm water. Sarah closed her eyes, leaned back, and rested her head against the back of the tub. She took a long, cleansing breath. Just as she was truly starting to relax, Mrs. Lee grabbed her hand and roughly scrubbed her arm with a brush and soap.

"Bath not place to sleep. Place to get clean."

Mrs. Lee proceeded to vigorously wash every inch of Sarah with a hard-bristled wooden brush. Sarah was jarred by the force of the scrubbing, first her neck, then her back and underarms. Mrs. Lee worked her way down until she even got between her toes. It felt as if the old woman might take off a layer of skin. But Sarah didn't want to upset her, so she didn't complain. She hadn't been bathed by anyone since her mother had done it when she was a little girl. Her mother had a much gentler hand. But it felt nice to be taken care of again, even if it was by a tough old Chinese woman she barely knew.

"You have brothers? Sisters?"

"No," Sarah replied.

"Any family?"

"An uncle."

"Where he?"

"Back in my country."

"Why you not go back to him?"

"I am not sure he would take me," Sarah said. "But also, he is not nice to girls."

"Lots of men not nice to girls. Mrs. Lee's husband not nice to girls. He left us when daughters just babies. Poof, gone like that. I have to learn fast. Raise daughters. Run house. Become landlady. Do everything. Never trust a man. Men not reliable. Also lots of mean men in world. They like to feel big by making women feel small."

Sarah hesitated before asking the next question.

"Is Maryk a mean man?"

"Maryk not mean," Mrs. Lee said. She considered the question for a moment before continuing. "Just sad."

"Why?"

"Don't know. Sometimes a person never talk about sadness, because it bring too much pain. You see it on their face. Maryk show sadness in his face."

Mrs. Lee massaged some soap into Sarah's scalp and through her matted and tangled hair.

"You look like Irish girl with all this red hair. Pretty color. You never see red hair on Chinese girl."

When she finally emerged from the tub, Sarah's skin tingled and she felt cleaner than she had ever been. Mrs. Lee handed her a simple cotton robe.

"Here, put this on until we wash clothes. I get tub for laundry."

Mrs. Lee stepped through a door at the back of the kitchen that Sarah assumed led to the backyard.

Sarah was just pulling on the robe when she heard the front door of the building open and people move down the hallway toward the kitchen. She hastily tied the robe closed just as a middle-aged black couple entered, carrying armloads of groceries in paper sacks. The man was short with dark skin and a long droopy mustache. The woman was taller, and lighter skinned, with her hair tucked under a yellow-and-green striped scarf. As soon as the man beheld Sarah, he dropped his groceries, sending several onions, apples, and carrots rolling across the floor.

"What the . . . ?"

"My Lord in heaven," the woman said. "There's a half-naked girl in the kitchen! Smitty, get out of here!"

The man quickly covered his eyes, turned, and fled back down the hall where he had come from.

"Who are you?" the woman asked Sarah.

It was the third time she had been asked that question over the past few hours, and she was still unsure how to respond.

"I'm Sarah," she said.

"Well, what in the name of sweet Jesus are you doing here?"

Mrs. Lee reentered, carrying a washboard and basin. "Oh, Miss Jean, you back already."

"Yes, we're back," she said, crossing her arms.

"This is Sarah," Mrs. Lee said. "She going to work here."

"She's going to be working here, huh?" Miss Jean said, looking the girl up and down. "You have a problem with the way Smitty and I tend to our duties?"

"She work in kitchen. You work in house. Different."

"You never mentioned the need for kitchen help before. You know my sister Mavis can cook and—"

"I keep that in mind. Now go find Sarah some old clothes. Hers are filthy dirty. Can't have naked girl in kitchen all day. And then show her to Maryk's room."

"Maryk's room?" Miss Jean said, raising an eyebrow.

"He sleep in basement. One week only. Now go."

Little Indian
on a Horse

MISS JEAN WENT TO AN UPSTAIRS storage closet to retrieve a small bag of old clothes that had once belonged to one of Mrs. Lee's daughters and then led Sarah to Maryk's room on the second floor. Sarah had never been so close to a person with such dark skin, and she stole glances at her as they moved down the hallway. Miss Jean caught her staring and stopped short.

"You got a problem?"

"N-no," Sarah stammered.

"Then why are you staring at me like I've got three heads?"

"I'm sorry. It is just . . . your skin is so dark."

"Oh, really," Miss Jean said, putting her hands on her hips.

"It's very beautiful," Sarah added.

"I like to think so," Miss Jean said.

"Are you from Africa?"

"Africa? Girl, my people are from Kansas City. And the last time I checked, it was in the United States of America."

"I did not mean to insult you," Sarah said, trying to make her voice sound as apologetic as possible.

"You'd better brush up on your geography."

Miss Jean continued down the hall until she came to the last apartment and knocked on the door. After a moment, they heard a cough, and Maryk called from inside.

"Hold on a second," he barked.

After some heavy-limbed shuffling, the door swung open and there was Maryk, dressed in just his pants, suspenders, and an undershirt. Sarah had only ever seen him in his uniform. She could smell the whiskey on his breath as soon as the air from the open door pushed out into the hall.

"I've got a delivery for you," Miss Jean said, nudging Sarah toward the door.

"Thank you, Mrs. Jean," Sarah said, gesturing to the clothes in her hand.

"They weren't my clothes to give. But you're welcome. And it's *Miss* Jean, not *Mrs.* Me and Smitty have been married for twenty years, but I like the sound of 'Miss Jean' because it keeps me feeling young."

"Thank you, Miss Jean," Sarah said.

"Yeah, well, you're welcome. I guess."

Miss Jean rolled her eyes and turned and walked back down the stairs to the first floor, muttering to herself. "Sweet Jesus . . . what is this house coming to?"

Maryk and Sarah stood awkwardly for a moment.

"This is yours?" Sarah asked.

"Ah, yeah," Maryk said, gesturing for her to enter. Sarah stepped inside. The room was small and dingy and faced the alley behind the building, so hardly any light came in through the lone window. The sparse furnishings included a bed, a pine dresser, a small wooden desk and chair, and a shelf filled with a few well-thumbed old books. A tiny sink was stuck to the wall next to the desk with a round mirror hanging above it.

A half dozen empty bottles of Golden Clover Irish Whiskey along with one full one were lined up along the top of the dresser, next to a framed sepia-toned photograph.

"Toilet's down at the end of the hall. Don't forget to put the lock on. Mrs. Lee don't think too much about knocking. I've just got to gather a few things and then go take a sleep in the basement."

"You sleep now?"

"When I'm on the night shift, I've got to do my sleeping during the day."

Maryk arranged his uniform on a hanger and packed some socks and shoes into a small bag. Sarah approached the dresser and examined the framed photograph, which showed a pretty, petite, dark-skinned woman with eyes like Maryk's and long braided hair standing on the back of a white horse. The woman wore a feather in her hair and a short buckskin skirt and blouse decorated with long strips of fringe. A tall man with a head of thick blond hair stood beside the horse, holding the reins. Sarah picked up the picture to look at it more closely.

"Put that down," Maryk snapped.

"I'm sorry." She replaced the photograph with a shaky hand.

"I didn't say you could paw my things, did I?"

"No . . . I just . . . the picture is nice."

"Yeah," Maryk grumbled, reaching over to straighten the frame. "But you can't just start touching anything you please. You understand?"

"Yes. I'm sorry."

"Well, just mind yourself."

After a moment, Sarah nodded toward the photograph. "Who is in the picture?"

Maryk looked down, almost shyly. "My parents."

"Your mother and father?"

"Yes."

It surprised Sarah to think of Maryk even having parents, never mind parents who seemed to be performers of some kind.

"They were in a play?"

"No. They both worked for Buffalo Bill Cody's Wild West show. You ever hear of Buffalo Bill where you're from?"

Sarah shook her head.

"He's got a big show that's kind of like a circus, but it's all stuff about the Wild West. Trick riders, sharpshooters, knife throwers, cowboys and Indians, that kind of thing. They always do a big parade with all sorts of western characters, and an Indian War battle reenactment as the grand finale."

"I don't understand what this is."

"The Indians and the white man, they had lots of wars over here. And Buffalo Bill kind of does a make-believe version of the war. You understand what 'make believe' means? It's when you pretend."

"A pretend war?"

Sarah shuddered, thinking of the bloody bodies of the men from her village on the night of the attack. She couldn't understand why anyone would want to pretend to have a war.

"It sounds strange when you say it like that. But it's really just like a stage play, only with lots of horses and guns going off. So I guess they were sort of like actors."

Sarah tried to see traces of Maryk in the two people in the photo. They seemed so different from him. Yet as she looked closer, she could tell that he was a combination of both, with the almond eyes and serious expression of his mother and the broad body and thick hair of his father.

"Your mother was an Indian?"

"That's right."

"So you are Indian too?"

"Part Indian. My mother was from the Dakota tribe. Lots of Dakota worked for Cody in those days. My father was a horse wrangler from Sweden. So I'm probably the only half-Dakota, half-Swede you're ever gonna meet."

"Is this why the man you work with called you a half-breed?"

Maryk's expression darkened and he leaned forward. Sarah pressed herself against the wall as his enormous shadow engulfed her.

"Don't ever use that word again, you hear?" His sour breath steamed into her face. "Only idiots like Johnson say things like that."

"I'm sorry," she stammered.

"It's just about the lowest thing you could call somebody like me. So don't use it. Ever."

"I won't," she said. Her eyes filled with tears.

Maryk gruffly gathered up his belongings, stopping to pluck the full bottle of whiskey off the top of the dresser along with the photograph. He opened the door but then turned back.

"And don't touch any of my things!"

He slammed the door closed.

It took several minutes for Sarah's heart to stop racing.

She noticed a lock on the inside that she quickly, but quietly, turned shut. As soon as the door was bolted, Sarah felt her body relax, as if she'd been tensing every muscle the entire time she had been in the apartment building and could finally unclench.

She changed into some of the clothes that Miss Jean had brought her and sat on the bed. Scanning the bookshelf, she read some of the strange titles: *Don Quixote*, *Moby-Dick*, *The Last of the Mohicans*, and *Aesop's Fables*.

On the top shelf sat a wooden box covered with a layer of dust, as if it hadn't been touched in years.

Sarah approached the shelf. Then she guiltily glanced around. She wanted to find out as much about Maryk as she could, because she still didn't trust him. Maybe the box held a gun or some other kind of weapon. She needed to know what was inside.

She stood on her tiptoes and reached up. But just as she grabbed the box, there was a loud rap on the door. Sarah dropped the box back on the shelf and spun around.

"You come now," Mrs. Lee's voice called through the door. "Need you to sweep upstairs floors before make meal."

Sarah awkwardly tripped over her feet as she stepped away from the shelf.

"Yes. I come," she said.

The Wok

SARAH SPENT THE NEXT few hours dusting and sweeping the upstairs floors. As she finished, she heard a sizzle. Then came a warm, savory smell that made her mouth water.

She followed her nose down the stairs to the first floor and entered the kitchen to find Mrs. Lee hurrying around, gathering ingredients for the evening meal. An oversized black steel pot shaped like a giant bowl sat on the stove top, flames licking the bottom. Another large pot filled with white rice simmered on the back burner. Piles of uncut carrots, onions, and broccoli were stacked on the counter beside a thick wooden chopping block. Mrs. Lee handed Sarah a cleaver and pointed to the vegetables.

"You chop. I cook. You chop vegetables before?"

Sarah nodded.

"Be careful not to cut self. Bloody fingers not taste good. Bring over to wok when you finish."

Sarah took the cleaver and moved to the counter. She recalled her mother holding her hands in just the right way. And the memory gave Sarah confidence as she grasped a carrot and chopped in a steady rhythm, curling her fingers to stay clear of the blade. Chop, chop, chop, chop. One, two, three, four. Chop, chop, chop, chop. One, two, three, four. She efficiently made her way through the pile of carrots, forming the cut pieces into a neat pile. Mrs. Lee nodded in approval, scooping up the carrots and tossing them into the wok with a sizzling hiss.

She gestured inside the sink, where there were two plucked chickens.

"Now take meat off bone and cut into pieces."

Sarah's eyes widened. She had never deboned a chicken before. When her family could afford one, her mother would cook it whole in a pot, so the meat would just naturally fall off and the skin and bones would become part of the broth.

Sarah held one of the cool, clammy birds, unsure of where to make the first cut.

"Something wrong?" Mrs. Lee said.

"No," Sarah said.

She didn't want to expose any weakness in her skills. So she took a deep breath and confidently started to cut away the meat, first chopping the chicken into quarters and then carefully separating the meat from the bone and cutting it into smaller cubes.

Mrs. Lee grunted approval and then turned back to her own work.

As Sarah fell into the familiar rhythm of cooking, she unconsciously started to hum one of her mother's old work songs about cooking chicken. Some of the words sprang into her mind: "We never waste a thing, not a thigh, a breast, or wing." The music emerged naturally from somewhere deep inside Sarah, the melody weaving into the rhythm of the work.

Mrs. Lee turned when she heard the humming, until Sarah finally noticed her staring and abruptly stopped.

"Don't stop," Mrs. Lee said. "I like music. Have Gramophone music box machine. Play Enrico Caruso. You know Caruso?"

Sarah shook her head.

Mrs. Lee sang a few off-key operatic bars. *"Ridi, Pagliaccio, sul tuo amore infranto!"*

Sarah giggled.

"Okay. I not good at singing," Mrs. Lee said, nodding. "You wait here."

Mrs. Lee exited the room, then returned carrying a strange-looking wooden machine with a hand crank and a huge horn sticking out of the top. She struggled to settle the heavy piece of equipment onto the kitchen table. As Mrs. Lee vigorously turned the crank, Sarah thought the machine might be used for grinding meat. But a moment later, she jumped back as the sound of an orchestra boomed out of the horn.

"You see," Mrs. Lee said. "Caruso!"

Sarah listened to the powerful sound of the man's voice, and the aching emotion of the melody. It reminded her of the prayers the men in her village used to chant on Saturday mornings.

Mrs. Lee returned to her work but swayed along to the melody.

Sarah continued removing the chicken meat from the bone and watched Mrs. Lee's strange little dance out of the corner of her eye. She felt her mouth curl up into a smile. She still wasn't quite sure what to make of these unusual people, but she felt safe in the kitchen with Mrs. Lee preparing the evening meal while Caruso serenaded them.

Sarah finished carving and dicing the chicken, and Mrs. Lee added it to the hottest part of the wok. The meat instantly blanched and then slowly browned and crisped along the edges. She mixed the entire contents together with a pile of bean sprouts, then emptied the dish into an enormous serving bowl, sprinkling a handful of sesame seeds on top.

Mrs. Lee handed Sarah a brass bell from a low shelf.

"Go to stairs and ring this," she said. "Then watch out."

"Watch out?"

"You'll see."

Sarah stood at the bottom of the stairs and rang the bell. Instantly, doors opened up and down the hall and multiple sets of feet stomped down the stairs. Two dozen Chinese people of all ages quickly brushed past Sarah and moved to the dining table. There were two families with young children, nearly a dozen men of varying ages, and a group of four young women. They all sat themselves around the table.

A stout Chinese woman in a green dress came down the stairs with her daughter, who looked to be about Sarah's age. The girl was small and thin, with long, beautiful, shiny black hair that she wore pulled back and tied with a blue ribbon.

The woman regarded Sarah suspiciously.

"Who are you?"

"Sarah."

"You a new boarder?"

Sarah wasn't sure what the word *boarder* meant.

"I work in the kitchen."

"What are you talking about?"

"With Mrs. Lee. I help clean and cook."

The woman's face darkened. "I will not stand for this!" she said.

Mrs. Fat

"YOU SHOULD NOT BE HERE!" the woman continued. "This is an outrage."

"Mama, calm down," the Chinese girl interjected.

"No. I won't calm down," the woman said, her face turning even redder with agitation. "Mrs. Lee, I demand to see you right now! Mrs. Lee!"

"What's all this noise?" Mrs. Lee said, emerging from the kitchen while wiping her hands on her apron. "I run rooming house, not beer hall."

"Why did you hire this girl to work in the kitchen when you promised you'd give work to my Bao Yu if there was any?"

The woman nodded to her daughter and then angrily crossed her arms. Both Sarah and the girl shifted uncomfortably.

"Mrs. Fat, I never promise job to nobody," Mrs. Lee said. "This is Maryk's niece."

"Maryk has a niece?"

"Yes. And she a good worker."

"My Bao Yu is a good worker too," Mrs. Fat said.

"Well, when you own building, you can hire who you want. I own building, I hire who I say. Now go, eat. Sarah, you come serve."

Mrs. Fat huffed, and she and her daughter moved into the other room.

Sarah followed Mrs. Lee down the hall, feeling even more self-conscious than before. Between Miss Jean's sister and Mrs. Fat's daughter, there seemed to be a small army of people who wanted the job that Sarah had taken.

Sarah was almost back to the kitchen when Maryk stepped into her path, coming up the basement stairs. They nearly collided, and navigated around each other awkwardly.

"Excuse me," she said.

"Hmph," he grunted as he passed.

Maryk walked into the front room and took the lone empty seat at the end of the table. He was dressed for work in his brown uniform, his hair carefully combed. Despite his neat appearance, Sarah detected a slight unsteadiness in his walk and a whiff of whiskey on his breath.

Mrs. Lee emerged from the kitchen carrying the bowl filled with the steaming chicken-and-vegetable dish.

"You get rice," she said to Sarah. "Before it turn cold."

Sarah retrieved the rice bowl and joined Mrs. Lee, circling the table behind her and spooning clumps of rice onto each plate. Mrs. Fat eyed Sarah suspiciously from her seat beside her daughter.

Sarah tried to catch Maryk's attention as she made her way around the room, to give him a small smile of thanks and to show him how well she had integrated herself into the work life of the house already. She was hoping for a sign of their alliance or friendship, particularly since she had just made at least one enemy in Mrs. Fat. Yet Maryk seemed uncomfortable as she scooped the rice onto his plate.

"Thanks," he grunted, without looking up at her.

Everyone at the table was speaking Chinese with the exception of Maryk, who ate silently, and the four young women, who sat together and practiced their rudimentary English. Maryk hungrily forked the food into his mouth without making eye contact with anyone.

Sarah noticed the four Chinese girls staring at her. Unlike Maryk, they wouldn't take their eyes off of her and she felt uncomfortable under their glares. One of the girls whispered something to the others and they giggled.

At last Sarah came to Mrs. Fat and her daughter. She scooped out a large spoonful of rice for Mrs. Fat, but at the last minute, Mrs. Fat nudged her own plate so the rice spilled onto the table.

"Clumsy girl!" Mrs. Fat said.

Blood rushed into Sarah's face and she froze as Mrs. Lee, Maryk, and everyone else at the table turned and looked up at her.

"Why don't you watch what you're doing?" Mrs. Fat continued.

"But I didn't do anything," Sarah said, the heat rising up her neck.

"Liar. You dumped Mrs. Lee's good food all over the table. We don't waste food here."

Mrs. Lee's eyes narrowed at Sarah. Maryk finally fixed his eyes on her, too. He seemed to be angry at her for causing a fuss.

"I am not a liar," Sarah said firmly.

"It was my fault." Bao Yu spoke up for the first time. Sarah turned to the girl in surprise. "I moved the plate by accident. I'm sorry, Mama."

Bao Yu used her spoon to scoop the rice onto her mother's plate.

"You expect me to eat rice that's been dumped on a table?"

"My table so clean, you don't need plate," Mrs. Lee said.

"It's okay, Mama. I'll eat that rice."

She switched plates with her mother. Mrs. Fat glared at her daughter.

Everyone began eating.

Bao Yu caught Sarah's eye and mouthed the word "Sorry," before turning to her own plate of food.

Grace

SARAH FOLLOWED MRS. LEE into the kitchen. Smitty and Miss Jean were already seated at the small kitchen table, setting out the platters of food that Mrs. Lee had reserved for them.

Smitty stood up. "Miss, I'd like to apologize for barging in on you earlier. I'm Miss Jean's husband, Mr. Smith."

He extended his hand and Sarah shook it.

"Sarah," she said.

"A pleasure, Miss Sarah." He bowed grandly. "You can call me Smitty. Just about everyone does."

"All right, Prince Charming, let the girl sit down and eat," Miss Jean said.

Mrs. Lee gestured for Sarah to join them. "Sit," she said.

Sarah sat at the table, and Smitty and Miss Jean joined hands and closed their eyes.

"Bless us, O Lord," Miss Jean said, "and these thy gifts, which we are about to receive, through Jesus Christ, our Lord. Amen."

"Praise Jesus. Amen," Smitty said.

They turned to Sarah, clearly waiting for her to chime in with a "praise Jesus" or "amen" of her own. Sarah looked toward Mrs. Lee, unsure what to do.

"She is Jewish person," Mrs. Lee said. "They don't have Jesus prayers."

"Is that right?" Miss Jean said, raising an eyebrow. "You don't look Jewish with that red hair."

"Nothing wrong with that," Smitty chimed in. "Just a little unusual is all."

"I don't have Jesus prayers either," Mrs. Lee said. "I am Buddhist person." She bowed her head toward the food on the table. "This food is the gift of the whole universe. Each morsel is a sacrifice of life. May I be worthy to receive it."

Mrs. Lee, Miss Jean, and Smitty looked to Sarah for a reaction. She had never recited the evening prayers at home. That had always been her parents' job. But she had committed the Hebrew words to memory and knew what they meant.

"*Baruch atah Adonai,*" she began tentatively. "*Eloheinu melech haolam, hamotzi lechem min ha-aretz.* Amen."

Sarah felt proud of herself that she had memorized the prayer, but then she stiffened as she discovered the others staring at her.

"It is a prayer thanking God for bread," she said.

"Amen to that," said Smitty.

"Praise Jesus," Miss Jean piped in under her breath.

"Enough religion," Mrs. Lee said. "We eat now."

Maryk had already left for the night shift by the time Sarah went to clear the dishes from the dining table. Back in the kitchen Mrs. Lee handed her an apron from a hook on the door and pointed to the sink, where the dishes were stacked two feet high.

Sarah spent the next hour and a half washing and drying the dishes and then scrubbing the wok and rice pot with a wire brush. When Miss Jean finished mopping the front room, she sat at the kitchen table and watched Sarah toiling at the sink. Sarah was certain that dish washing had been Miss Jean's job before her arrival, and she knew her skills were being judged.

When the final pot was washed, she felt Miss Jean tap her on the shoulder. Sarah spun around, afraid she had made a mistake.

"I'll show you where they go," Miss Jean said, nodding with some admiration.

She helped Sarah put everything away.

"Well, you're not afraid of rolling up your sleeves and getting your hands dirty. Come here. I'll help you with that."

She gestured for Sarah to turn around and then untied her apron, lifted it over her head, and hung it on the back of the door.

"Thank you," Sarah said.

"It was nothing," Miss Jean replied.

"Breakfast served at seven thirty," Mrs. Lee said, reentering the room. "You come down at six thirty to cook with me. You understand?"

"Yes." Sarah nodded. "And thank you. Thank you both."

"You go to sleep now," Mrs. Lee said. "You look like you been run over by wagon."

A Real Bed

As soon as Sarah stepped into Maryk's room, her body went slack as the remaining energy drained out of her. It had been more than a full day since she had last slept in the crown room of the Lady and several weeks since she had lain in a proper bed. She felt as if she had lived an entire lifetime since leaving her village. In her one day in Manhattan, she had seen and heard more new and strange things and people than she would have in an entire lifetime back home.

Sarah wasn't sure what to make of any of the new people she had met. Maryk, Mrs. Lee, Miss Jean and Smitty, Mrs. Fat and Bao Yu were all so different from her or anyone she had ever known, and she had trouble figuring out whom she could trust. She longed to talk to her mother or father to help guide her. She had been so busy during the day that she had been distracted from her grief. But now, alone in Maryk's room, she missed them more than ever.

She turned the lock on the door and sat on the bed, where she removed her boots and coat and finally lay down. Her body sank into the soft mattress and pillow, a welcome sensation after all the hard surfaces she had been forced to sleep on.

She removed Ivan from the pocket of her skirt and placed him on the pillow beside her.

"It feels like we're lying on a cloud," she whispered to the bear.

Sarah recognized the slightly sour smell of Maryk on the sheets and pillow. But she was too overwhelmed with exhaustion to mind. Her muscles relaxed, her bones settling into the cushiony surface. Her eyes fluttered shut and she fell into a deep sleep.

Sarah dreamed she was cutting vegetables the same way that she had just done for Mrs. Lee. But now she was back in her little house in her village, staring out the window into their family garden.

Sarah's mother appeared behind her, singing a clear lilting melody, and deposited a few potatoes beside her on the table. She patted Sarah gently on the shoulder. The warmth of the touch made Sarah's body tingle.

Sarah heard a chopping sound and looked out the window to see her father standing beside the woodpile. He raised a small hand ax high over his head and brought it down to split a log that sat on a large stump they used for chopping. He glanced up at Sarah and his mouth creased into a smile, crow's-feet sprouting next to his eyes. Then he turned his attention back to the wood, raised the ax, and chopped. The log splintered in two with a loud crack.

Sarah jolted awake. She sat up in the darkness of Maryk's room unsure of where she was, still trapped in the warm fantasy of the dream. Then she heard another sharp noise coming from the hallway just outside the door. A cold shiver shot through her. Someone was fiddling with the lock.

Midnight Intruder

SARAH AUTOMATICALLY REACHED for Ivan and shoved him back in her pocket. Afraid to move, she held her breath as she heard the sound of a key struggling to find its way into the metal hole. The key clattered to the floor and she heard Maryk's muffled voice through the door.

"Ugh," he grunted with exertion as he bent to pick it up. A moment later, the knob turned.

Sarah suddenly remembered her father's scissors. She grabbed the coat that she had laid across the end of bed and patted down the front until she found the small hard lump in the inner pocket. She pulled out the scissors. The blades were thin and very sharp. She gripped the weapon tightly and pushed herself into an upright position, her back against the wall.

The door swung open and Maryk's dark shadow fell into the room. His tall, hulking frame paused in the doorway for a moment, swayed, then stepped inside and closed the door. Sarah could not see his face, but she could hear his heavy breathing and smell the sour odor of whiskey and pipe tobacco.

Sarah's entire body shook as she held the scissors in front of her, bracing for his attack. She gripped the scissors tighter as he walked unsteadily forward. His shadow slowly crept over her, casting her in deeper darkness. When he was nearly to the bed, she thrust the scissors toward him.

"Don't come any closer!"

He recoiled and stopped, as if surprised by her presence.

"What the . . . ," he sputtered.

"What are you doing here?"

"What am I doing here? It's my room, ain't it?" His tongue was thick and slowed by whiskey.

"You said I could stay here."

"I did?" he growled.

"Yes. You did."

He swayed on his feet.

"I just came to get something is all."

"It is the middle of the night. . . ."

"Man's got a right to get something out of his own room. . . ."

"Can't you get it in the morning?"

He stood in the darkness for a long moment, his labored breathing the only sound.

"Please . . . ," she added.

Finally he veered off toward the dresser and reached for one of the bottles of whiskey, accidentally knocking some of them to the floor with a loud crash.

"Criminy!" he growled.

Sarah jumped but still held the scissors out before her.

"They are all empty," she said.

"Huh?"

"There is no whiskey in them. You already took the last full one."

Maryk kicked one of the empty bottles, causing it to ricochet off the wall.

"You can have your room back."

"Huh?"

"I can go sleep in the basement," she said, her voice trembling. "Just please. Don't hurt me."

He took a deep breath and pointed an angry finger at her. "You stay right there!"

Then he turned and walked out of the room, slamming the door as he went.

Sarah loosened her grip on the scissors until they dropped out of her hand and onto the bed. Her heart beat furiously, the blood coursing through her until her head felt like it would burst.

After that, Sarah couldn't sleep. Was Maryk really just hunting for more whiskey? What if he came back and tried to attack her? And even if he meant her no harm and left her alone, what was she going to do to survive on her own? Mrs. Lee had only agreed to let her stay one week. She needed to find a way to make money quickly, so she could get away from these strange people and find her own place to live.

Sarah knew there were other immigrants from her country, probably from her village, in New York City. She just needed to find them. As soon as possible, she would track down her people and get a job as buttonhole maker just like she and her mother had intended. Gripping her father's scissors in her hand, Sarah felt as if she was holding on to her protection and her future all at once.

Fifteen Holes per Hour

AFTER CLEANING UP FROM breakfast the next morning, Sarah wandered in and around the twisting streets of Chinatown. She saw two older Jewish men, in dark suits and white beards, and hurried up to walk close behind them so she could overhear their conversation in Yiddish.

"The price of wool just keeps going up," one said.

"It's like there's a shortage of sheep out there," the other agreed.

They must be in the garment business, Sarah reasoned. So she decided to follow them.

Sure enough, within a few blocks the store signs turned from Chinese to Hebrew and Yiddish and the streets were filled with people who came from her country. Pushcarts lined the sidewalks selling all sorts of familiar wares and foods like braided rolls and knishes stuffed with meat and potato. She wished she had some money to buy herself a taste of home.

Sarah came to a street where huge rolls of fabric stuffed into barrels lined the sidewalks in front of the buildings. Burly men pulled various bolts and carried them inside. Other men with tape measures draped around their necks ducked in and out of doorways, examining fabrics and threads. Seeing these men reminded her of her father, who also used to go to work armed with a tape measure in addition to his precious scissors. Farther along, she passed another man mixing a large vat of deep crimson fabric dye.

A group of girls passed by on the street, speaking her native language. Sarah leaned toward them as they strolled by, hungry to pick up any snippets of their conversation.

She longed to fall into the group and follow them, wherever they were going, to be talking about something as simple as what they ate for lunch, to feel a part of something familiar again.

These are my people, she thought. *Not Maryk, Miss Jean, and Mrs. Lee.*

Sarah paused by a window where she could see a huge room filled with women and girls working at sewing machines. Toward the back of the room, she caught a glimpse of a group of women bent low over garments. Her eyes widened and she moved closer as she realized that they were making buttonholes. Maybe there was work for her too.

A tall man in a suit with a neatly trimmed beard walked among the rows, checking the girls' work. Sarah assumed he was the boss.

She gave Ivan a squeeze inside her pocket for good luck and entered the factory. A few of the garment workers glanced up at Sarah as she approached the bearded man.

"Excuse me, sir," she said.

He turned to her with a cross expression.

"Who let you in here?"

"No one. I just came in. I am looking for a job."

"Who isn't?" he said.

"I'm a buttonhole maker," she said.

"I have plenty of those."

She stood up straighter. "I was the best in my village."

A few of the women making buttonholes glanced up at her doubtfully.

"How many holes can you make an hour?" one asked.

Sarah had never really counted. But, in truth, she knew she wasn't very fast. She lied.

"Fifteen," she said.

"Fifteen!" The women laughed. "We do at least twenty-five."

"I can do thirty if I've had a good night's sleep," another said.

"My record's thirty-nine," a third chimed in.

"All right, back to work," the man with the beard said. "We're not hiring now anyway. I'm sorry."

"But . . ."

"Look, miss, we really have to get back to work."

Then Sarah remembered her scissors. She quickly pulled them out of her pocket.

"I have my own scissors," she said, holding them up. "They're very fine. See! So I wouldn't even have to use one of yours."

The man paused and took the scissors from her hand. The other women nodded and whispered to each other, impressed. He held the scissors up and examined them.

"These are good. Professional," the man said. He handed them back. "Work on your speed and come back in three weeks. Maybe one of these experts will have retired."

"What? And leave all this glamour behind?" one of the women joked. The others laughed.

"But I don't have three weeks," Sarah said. "I need to make money now."

"Sorry, kid," the man said. "That's the best I can do."

Sarah felt deflated as she walked back out onto the street. It didn't really matter how many holes she could sew after all. She'd have to come up with a new plan.

She started to head back to Mrs. Lee's when she felt a hand tap her on the shoulder. She spun around and was startled to discover one of the older women who had been in the garment factory. The woman had long gray hair tied under a blue kerchief and kind eyes. Sarah braced herself to run, afraid she was going to be threatened by the woman for trying to take her job.

"Hey, it's all right," the woman said in Yiddish. "I just wanted to tell you, if you're really in a pinch for money, there are places that will hire you."

Sarah looked up, hope swelling inside her again.

"Can you tell me where?"

"There's one not too far from here, at one eleven Essex Street."

"One eleven Essex," Sarah repeated.

"Yes, but you should be careful. Some of those places aren't so nice. And you've gotta watch out for the bosses. They can be trouble."

"What kind of trouble?"

"All kinds. Just be careful. Good luck to you. And God bless you."

As the woman went back inside the garment factory, Sarah repeated the address to herself again, so she wouldn't forget it. She slowly walked to Mrs. Lee's, weighed down by worries about her now-uncertain future. Would anyone really hire her?

Smitty and Miss Jean

"WHERE HAVE YOU BEEN?"

Miss Jean stood by the front door with her hands on her hips as Sarah entered the hall.

"Oh, I was just out walking around," Sarah said.

"Well, it was my understanding that you were working for Mrs. Lee now, so you should let us know if you're planning on going anywhere."

"I'm sorry. I will."

"As long as you've got your coat on, you can leave it on and come out with me. Mrs. Lee asked me to pick up some things for the evening meal. I could use an extra set of hands. Smitty's out back fixing the drain. Go ask him if he needs any pipe tobacco while we're out and then meet me in the front hall."

Sarah discovered Smitty in the backyard, leaning against a shovel beside a freshly dug hole. As she approached, Sarah saw that the hole revealed some exposed pipes in the ground and Smitty was reading from a set of plans that seemed to be a map of some kind.

"Hello there," he said, glancing up at her. "We've got a blocked pipe somewhere out here that's making all the sinks back up. I'm just trying to figure out which one it is."

None of the homes in Sarah's village had running water, and she was fascinated by the advanced plumbing system that seemed to be in place at Mrs. Lee's.

"Would you believe, I drew up these plans myself and now I can't make sense of them."

"You made this?" she asked with surprise.

"Studied engineering at Tuskegee. Class of ninety."

"You are an engineer?"

"By education if not in practice. Most of the time I'm dedicated to the janitorial arts." He wryly chuckled.

"What is that?"

"Means I fix and clean things up around here. Turns out there weren't many opportunities at engineering firms for people of my particular shade."

"Shade?"

"My skin color, dear. You don't meet many Negro engineers."

"Why?" Sarah said.

His expression turned serious.

"I'm afraid that one-word question has a long, complicated, and not very good answer."

Sarah genuinely wondered what about his skin would make someone not want him to be an engineer. America seemed to be full of people of different colors.

"What can I do for you?" he said.

"Miss Jean and I are going out and she wanted me to ask you if you need any more tobacco."

"That's awfully considerate of you both. But I think I'm all set for now."

Sarah returned inside and found Miss Jean waiting for her in the front hall, putting on her coat and scarf. "Ah, there you are," she said.

"He said he did not need any tobacco."

"All right."

Sarah watched as Miss Jean stared into a round, framed mirror by the door and put on a wide-brimmed, navy-blue felt hat with a sharp little brown feather sticking up out of the band. Miss Jean glimpsed Sarah out of the corner of her eye.

Sarah quickly looked away.

"You really have got to control that habit of staring at people," Miss Jean said.

"Sorry," she said.

Miss Jean paused and then went into the closet and retrieved a gray felt hat with a red band and a small silk flower attached to the side.

"Here, try this one. It's cold out there."

Sarah placed the hat on her head and Miss Jean pulled it down into the proper position.

"Not bad," Miss Jean said, turning Sarah toward the mirror.

Sarah stared at her reflection and almost didn't recognize

herself. The hat seemed to have transformed her into a different person, someone older and more American. She smiled shyly at herself.

"Don't get too used to it. It's just a loan. Now come on."

Village of Men

THEY MADE THEIR WAY toward Mott Street, the main thoroughfare of the neighborhood. People bustled around them, purposefully weaving along the street and sidewalk in a way that reminded Sarah of densely packed ants moving in purposeful patterns in the dirt mounds in her old backyard.

Miss Jean stopped at a vegetable vendor and purchased a sack of carrots and a large bag of bean sprouts that the man pulled from a metal tub filled with water. Next, she moved on to another stall that sold spices and rice out of huge open barrels. A Chinese man with a thin black beard approached.

"Five-pound bag today, Miss Jean?"

"Better make it seven," she said.

He dipped a small hand shovel into a barrel of white rice and scooped several pounds into a cloth sack.

"I see you've got a new assistant," he said.

"Yeah, Smitty had to work around the house."

"Nice to see another girl in the neighborhood," he said, handing

Sarah the bag in exchange for some coins Miss Jean had extracted from her purse. "You're a rare breed around here."

"I've always been a rare breed," Miss Jean said.

"That's the truth." The man laughed.

"What did he mean, 'rare breed'?" Sarah asked as Miss Jean led her away. "Is it the same as half-breed?" Sarah asked.

"No. They're very different things. How'd you know that word?"

"Someone called Maryk that."

"'Half-breed' is a nasty way of saying someone has a mixed background, that they're not one specific color. A rare breed is something special."

"What makes you special?"

"Well, lots of things," Miss Jean said. "But what he was talking about was the fact that we're women."

"I don't understand," Sarah said.

"Look around you," Miss Jean said. "What do you see?"

"People."

"What kind of people?"

"Chinese people," Sarah tentatively guessed.

"Chinese *men*," Miss Jean said, gesturing to the crowds around them. "There aren't a whole lot of ladies in this part of town. All the immigrants who come over from China are men, because they're the ones who can get jobs. You don't see nearly any Chinese girls down here, so you and I are minorities in more ways than one. You're lucky you found your way to Mrs. Lee. She collects stray cats like you. Those Chinese girls she has living at the house, they're orphans or escaped from all sorts of very bad situations. Lord knows what would've happened to them if Mrs. Lee hadn't taken them in. And old Mrs. Fat and her girl, Bao Yu, they'd be all alone too."

"What happened to Bao Yu's father?"

"He was a merchant, but he died a couple of years ago. They lost nearly everything. Like I said, hard to think about what would've happened to them if it wasn't for Mrs. Lee."

They made their way back toward the apartment building. They were just about to turn onto Pell Street when a voice called, "Hold it right there!" Sarah froze in place, unsure if the voice was calling to her. Miss Jean walked on, unaware. Sarah heard the voice again.

"Yeah, you, Red!"

The hair stood up on the back of Sarah's neck. She was being watched.

Tommy Grogan

SARAH SLOWLY TURNED TO see who was calling to her. Should she run?

"Right here," the voice said.

Sarah looked down and beheld a small, thin boy, who couldn't have been more than eleven years old, carrying a newspaper in one hand with a bag full of them slung over his shoulder. His ragged clothing hung off of his bony frame, and a big, floppy wool cap sat on his head at a slant.

"You wanna buy a paper, Red?"

"A paper?"

"Yeah, the *New York World*. I got all the dirt about what's going on all over the city."

"Dirt?" She furrowed her brow in confusion. "Why would I want to read about dirt?"

The boy laughed. "*Dirt*'s just a way of saying 'the news you want to read about.' Wow, you must've just fallen off the boat, huh?"

Sarah grinned, amused by the boy and his brash way of talking. She resisted the urge to tell him that she hadn't *fallen* off the boat, she jumped.

"With that hair, I thought you were Irish, like me. You ever been to County Cork?"

"No."

"So what's a redhead like you doin' in Chinatown?"

"I'm staying with my uncle."

"You got a Chinese uncle?"

"No, he's not Chinese."

"Well, does your uncle read the papers? Only a penny."

Up ahead, Miss Jean stopped, looked back, and called, "Sarah, come along now!"

The boy regarded Miss Jean with surprise.

"Who's that? Your aunt? You've got a Negro aunt and a Chinese uncle?"

"She's not my aunt," Sarah said. "And I told you he's not Chinese."

"Well, one of them must read the papers. Come on, I need to make a sale. Mr. Duffy expects me to sell this whole stack by sundown."

The boy held out his hand, and something in his expression changed.

"Please," he said in a more serious tone. "A guy's gotta eat, you know."

"I don't have a penny with me," she said, feeling sorry for the boy. "But I'll try to find one for tomorrow."

Miss Jean stood impatiently with her hands on her hips. "Sarah!" she snapped.

"I've got to go," Sarah said.

"Okay. But be sure to buy from me, Tommy Grogan," he said, the bravado returning to his voice. "The best newsie in all of lower Manhattan."

"I will," she said.

He grandly offered his hand. She tentatively extended hers and they shook.

"See you later, Red."

Sarah rejoined Miss Jean, who shook her head.

"You'd better wash that hand real good," Miss Jean said. "Half of those newsies live in flea-ridden flophouses. The other half live on the streets. I bet that boy hasn't had a proper bath all year."

Sarah glanced back over her shoulder and saw Tommy's small hand lifting a paper above the crowd and heard his voice calling, "Get your *New York World* here. Only a penny!"

When Sarah arrived back at Maryk's room, she hesitated before opening the door. Would Maryk be inside? She decided to knock, just in case, but there was no answer. She put her ear to the door to listen but heard no sound from within. Was he passed out on the bed? Or trying to trick her into thinking he wasn't there when he really was? She took a deep breath and opened the door.

The Other Photograph

SARAH PEEKED HER HEAD inside the room and exhaled as she discovered it was empty. She closed and locked the door.

Stepping over to the shelf, she scanned Maryk's small collection of books. She plucked out *Aesop's Fables* and flipped through the well-worn pages, stopping short when she came to the story titled "Androcles and the Lion." Maryk had called her that name on the first night they spoke on the Lady's island.

As Sarah read the fable, she couldn't help but smile, picturing herself as the slave and Maryk as the ferocious lion. She quickly skimmed through the rest of the collection.

Maryk had underlined many sentences and put check marks beside some:

Injuries may be forgiven, but not forgotten.

A liar will not be believed, even when he speaks the truth.

One passage in particular was underlined and annotated with a large question mark:

Try as one may, it is impossible to deny one's nature.

The words were somewhat mysterious to Sarah, but she assumed that they were important to Maryk. It was hard for her to think of the gruff, hard-drinking giant as a man who read books and attempted to find meaning in them.

She replaced the book, her attention wandering to the wooden box on the top shelf. She self-consciously glanced back over her shoulder, remembering Maryk's stern warning not to touch his things. But her curiosity overcame her hesitation, and she carefully pulled down the box.

Brushing off the top layer of dust revealed a chessboard pattern painted on the lid. Sarah's father had taught her how to play, another unusual skill he had passed on to his daughter. She remembered his pride as she mastered the game and was eventually able to defeat many of the boys in their town. Boys and men from other villages would come to see her demonstrate her skills, as if watching a cow that could talk.

Sarah sat down on the bed and opened the box. Inside was a set of simple wooden chess pieces. Running her fingers along the neat row of figures, she noticed a brown envelope tucked under them and slid it out. Peeking inside, she found a small, worn photograph of a pretty young woman with long, neatly styled dark hair and skin. She removed the photo to get a better look. The woman held an infant on her lap dressed in a long, frilly white gown and a ribbon in her hair.

Before she had a chance to study the photograph too closely, a loud knock came at the door that so startled Sarah, she abruptly sat up and knocked the chess set from the bed, spilling the pieces across the floor.

"What was that?" Maryk called from outside the door.

"N-nothing . . . ," she stammered.

Sarah fell to her knees to pick up the scattered pieces.

"I told you not to touch anything!"

"Yes, I know. . . ."

She quickly shoveled the pieces back into the box.

"I'm coming in," he said.

"Wait . . . I . . ."

Before Sarah could find the words to hold him off, the key turned in the lock and the door swung open. Still on her knees, Sarah glanced up.

"What do you think you're doing?" Maryk asked.

"I was just . . ."

"You were just what? Didn't I tell you not to touch my things?"

"I was just going to use the chessboard."

"You should ask before you take."

"I know," she said, fear running through her. "I'm sorry."

"I came up here to apologize for barging in last night," he said, his voice rising with anger. "But I guess I should've been keeping a closer watch on you."

"I am sorry," she said again, picking up more pieces and placing them in the box.

"I'm the one who's sorry for trusting you."

"Please, I didn't mean to do anything wrong. I just wanted to play chess."

She got to her feet.

Maryk's eyes suddenly fixed on the bed, where the photograph lay exposed next to its brown envelope. His expression hardened into a pinched scowl. Sarah followed his glance, and her throat tightened as he made his way toward the bed. She felt a deep shame at having disobeyed him and violated his trust.

For a long moment, he just looked down at the photograph. Sarah watched him, afraid that he might strike her at any moment and bracing for the blow. Finally he reached down and picked up the photograph.

Maryk sat on the bed, cradling the photograph in his thick palm. His entire body seemed to deflate. Sarah stood in the middle of the room, holding the chess set, unsure what to say or do. There was something unsettling about watching someone so physically imposing become so suddenly shriveled. Yet she also felt an unexpected pang in her chest.

She moved tentatively toward him. Maryk didn't look up, even as she stood directly beside him.

"Is that your wife?" she said.

"None of your business," he snapped.

He stood and tucked the photograph into the inside pocket of his jacket. Sarah backed away, frightened by his sudden outburst.

"And for the last time, keep your hands off my things."

He abruptly exited, slamming the door as he went.

111 Essex Street

LATE THE NEXT MORNING, Sarah stood on the sidewalk looking up at the imposing brick building. A small plaque over the door read 111 ESSEX STREET, but other than that there were no signs or indications that there might be a garment factory or any other business there. The windows were made from frosted glass and smeared with dirt, so she couldn't see what was going on inside.

Her run-ins with Maryk over the past couple of days had left her shaken about how much she could trust or rely on him. So she took a deep breath and opened the door, revealing a long, dark stairwell leading to the second floor. Sarah climbed the stairs and reached a battered steel door with a small sliding panel that served as a peephole. Pausing, she pressed her ear against the door but couldn't hear anything distinct.

Something about the place made the hairs on the back of her neck stand up, and she thought about turning back. But this seemed like her only hope of finding a real job.

Sarah checked her pocket for her scissors and knocked. After a moment a voice called from inside. "Who is it?"

"I'm looking for work," she said. "I'm a buttonhole maker."

The panel in the door slid open and an eye peered out at her.

"I heard you might have work," she said. "I have my own scissors."

She took the scissors out of her pocket and held them up for the eye to see. The panel abruptly shut, and then there was silence. Sarah was about to put the scissors back in her pocket and go when she heard the heavy metal locks turning and the door opened.

"Come in," the voice said.

She stepped inside and he quickly shut the door. The man was younger than Sarah had expected him to be, not much older than a teenager. He was thin with a high forehead and black hair that was combed in a sharp part down the middle. The room was filled with rows of women and girls all bent over garments. Unlike the other factory, no one was talking or even looked up when she entered.

"Let's see the scissors," the man said.

Sarah reluctantly handed them to him.

"Not bad," he said, examining them. He didn't hand them back. "You ever work in a factory before?"

Sarah hesitated, but then shook her head.

"That's all right. I might be able to find you something. Do you know how to stitch?"

She wasn't much of a seamstress, but she figured she had to try.

"Yes. But I'm really a buttonhole maker."

"Don't have any need for that this week," he said.

Sarah looked around the room. Some of the girls looked no more than eleven years old. Another man walked among the rows of workers watching over them like a guard. One young girl with sad eyes glanced up at Sarah but then quickly looked down. Again, she felt a chill run down her back.

"If you can stitch, I can use you. I've got a deadline on a job, so I need an extra set of hands. I've got twelve hours to get it all done. So why don't you take a seat over there, and one of the other girls will show you what to do."

"All right," Sarah said. She was about to walk over and join the others, but she paused, mustering up her courage. "Can I have my scissors back, please?"

"I think I'll hold on to them for you," he said with smile. "I wouldn't want you to misplace such a fine pair while you're working."

Sarah glanced around the room again. The same little girl was looking up at her and gave her a quick shake of the head. The man supervising the workers noticed the girl had stopped stitching. "Get back to work," he said, pinching the back of her arm. The girl grimaced and returned to her work.

Sarah knew then that the man in charge had no intention of giving her scissors back.

"Go on and start working," he said. "I've got a hard deadline."

The man moved to put the scissors into his pocket. Sarah instinctively shot out her hand and snatched them.

"Hey," he said, his face darkening with agitation and surprise.

"What do you think you're doing?"

"That's all right," she said, backing away. "I don't really need the work right now."

He took a step toward her.

"Get back here," he said.

She quickly turned and bolted out the door and down the stairs. As she fled, his voice called after her. "You'll be back. Who else is going to hire someone like you?"

Partners

SARAH TOSSED AND TURNED all that night, worried that Maryk might pay another unexpected visit or that she had angered him so much that he would kick her out of the building. And then where would she go? She couldn't imagine going back to 111 Essex Street. But how else could she make any real money?

At breakfast, he didn't even glance at her once as she came around pouring the coffee and delivering oatmeal. And she grew even more unsettled.

As she dried the final breakfast dish, Mrs. Lee approached her, carrying a blue leather change purse.

"I need you to run errand for me. Buy newspapers. Get three—two for people in house to share, one for me."

Mrs. Lee handed Sarah three pennies. "Mrs. Lee like to read all the bad news before bed," she said. "Make me feel better to know some people have it worse."

Sarah put on her coat and headed west through Chinatown. She passed several newsies on each street corner, but she wanted to find Tommy Grogan and give him her business like she had promised.

"Get your *New York World*!"

Sarah's ears perked up as she heard Tommy calling out above the street noise.

"All the dirt, only a penny!"

She followed the sound of his voice to the end of the block, where she found him in his floppy wool hat, holding up his papers and trying to interest people as they walked by.

"Jewel thieves terrorize the shops of Broadway!" he called. "Read all about it. Shopkeepers looted by gangs in broad daylight!"

Sarah approached him.

"Hey, Red!" he said. "You ready to buy a paper?"

"I'll take three," she said, handing him the pennies.

"Thanks," he said.

He gave her three papers from his bag. "Feels good to lighten the load a little."

Sarah noticed Tommy rehoisting the heavy bag onto his shoulder and she had an idea.

"Do you need help?"

"What do you mean?"

"Well, if I carry your bag, you could probably move faster and sell more. I need to make money and you need the help. I have time after I clean up from breakfast and lunch."

"I'm not sure Mr. Duffy would want me to," he said.

"Who's Mr. Duffy?"

"He's kind of like my boss. But we take care of each other."

"Do you really think he'd mind?"

"Well, I guess I could use an assistant. And the more I sell, the more I make."

"With me helping, you'd sell a lot more than you do now."

Tommy paused, considering the offer.

"Okay," he finally said. "We can give it a try."

He spit into his palm and held out his hand. She recoiled.

"Why did you spit on yourself?"

"To seal the deal. We both spit and shake on it to make it stick. You in?"

She looked at his hand and then tentatively spit into hers and shook.

"It is a deal," she said. "I've got to bring these back and finish my chores. But I'll come find you tomorrow."

"Okay, partner," Tommy said, tipping his cap. The word "partner" filled Sarah with a new sense of hope.

Checkmate

AFTER DELIVERING THE PAPERS to Mrs. Lee, Sarah entered the parlor and was surprised to discover Maryk sitting at the table. And even more surprised to see him freshly shaven, dressed in relatively clean clothing, and setting up the pieces on his chess set. He was wiping off each piece with a handkerchief.

"Since you already messed around with it, I thought I'd take it out and dust it off," Maryk said.

"I can help," Sarah said, tentatively. "If you want me to."

"Sure," he grunted. "Why not."

She went to the kitchen and retrieved a rag and returned to the parlor. Sitting across from Maryk, she started to wipe off and set up pieces on her side of the board. They worked in silence until all the pieces were clean and the board set for action.

"You know how to play?"

"Yes." Sarah nodded. "My father taught me."

"Well, back in my circus days, I was known as a bit of a chess shark."

"A fish that plays chess?" She cocked her head doubtfully.

"A shark, not a fish. Sharks are killers. That means I was good. Real good."

Sarah nodded. "I am good too."

"Oh, yeah?" he said.

"Best in my village," she said, unable to suppress a grin.

"Never played a girl before."

"I have never played a shark before."

Maryk gestured for her to make the first move. She slid one of her pawns forward. Just a few moves into the game, Sarah took one of his pawns and then another. Maryk squinted at the board.

"Hmmm," he grunted.

An old Chinese man who lived in the building entered the room and stood beside the table, silently watching with his hands behind his back. Maryk shifted uncomfortably in his seat and made his next move. The Chinese man frowned. Sarah quickly moved one of her pieces and captured another pawn.

Smitty walked in the front door and noticed the game in progress.

"What do we have here?"

He stood beside the Chinese man and examined the board.

"Oh, I see what she's doing," Smitty said, nodding his head. "Not a bad strategy."

"Don't know how anyone's supposed to concentrate with all this chatter going on," Maryk snapped.

He made another move but kept his hand on the piece, glancing up at Sarah to gauge her reaction. She raised an eyebrow but made sure he wouldn't be able to tell if she was impressed or disapproved of his move. He finally pulled back his hand and moved another piece. Sarah instantly captured one of his knights.

"Drat," Maryk muttered.

Sarah smiled.

Bao Yu and two of the other Chinese girls also wandered in. Bao Yu stood at the back but watched Sarah's every move with interest. Maryk fidgeted in his seat.

Within a dozen moves Sarah had taken a rook, the second knight, and both bishops, while Maryk had barely collected a few of her pieces. Finally, she had him trapped.

"Check," she said.

He gruffly moved his queen.

Sarah made one more move, feeling the thrill of victory rise up in her chest.

"Checkmate." She smiled.

Maryk slammed his hand on the table, scattering the pieces on the board. Sarah jerked as a rook and a bishop fell into her lap. Some of the spectators took a step back.

"I haven't played in years," he said. "Just out of practice is all."

"I'll give her a game," Smitty chimed in.

"No," Maryk snapped. "I want a rematch."

"Rematch?" Sarah said.

"Another game," he said impatiently. "Now set up the pieces."

After a moment, she warily reset the board.

When the pieces were in place, he gruffly slid a pawn forward. A few moves into the game, Maryk captured one of her pieces.

"Ha," he said. "I won't lie down so easy this time."

A few more moves and he captured another piece. And then a third. He was about to capture another when he paused and looked at Sarah's face. She stared at the board, biting her bottom lip. He leaned back and sighed.

"Play it straight," he said.

"What?" she said.

"I said play it straight!"

He wiped the pieces off the board in one swift motion. Everyone gasped. Sarah stood up and backed away from the table.

"I know what you're doing," he said, leaning toward her. "Now, play to win or I'm gonna get even madder. You understand?"

She nodded slowly.

"All right then," he said. And he began to reset the pieces to start a new game.

"My move," he said.

They started a third game. This one was played more evenly. But Sarah eventually had him trapped again.

"Checkmate," she said, and then held her breath, waiting for the explosion.

Maryk just grunted and stood up.

"I know when I'm licked," he said.

He stepped back away from the table. Sarah exhaled.

Bao Yu smiled at Sarah, clearly impressed.

"You up for another game?" Smitty gestured to the board.

Sarah nodded.

"Then I guess I'm the next lamb to the slaughter," Smitty said. "But I'm warning you, girl, I'm a smart old lamb. I was school champ at Tuskegee for three years running."

Smitty was a more formidable opponent. Sarah took longer pauses between moves and considered her strategy carefully.

At first, Maryk stood back with his arms tightly crossed, still smarting from his defeat. But as the game progressed, he moved closer to the other spectators.

Smitty played aggressively, capturing several of her important pieces. Sarah battled back, matching his daring moves until she had him trapped.

"Checkmate," Sarah said.

Smitty shook his head with a resigned grin, rose from the chair, and saluted her.

"You got me this time, Miss Sarah. But I'll get you the next one."

The spectators clapped. Bao Yu applauded the loudest, but then seemed to catch herself and stopped.

Sarah felt her face flush from all the attention. But as she looked around at the people applauding for her, she felt, for the first time, a true sense of belonging.

"That's my chess set," Maryk said to no one in particular.

Mrs. Lee entered the room, drawn in by the noise.

"What goes on in here? I thought I hired worker, not chess hustler. You come help in kitchen now."

The News Business

THE NEXT MORNING SARAH'S eyes darted left and right as she wound through the streets searching for Tommy. She finally found him, calling out his headlines on the corner of Canal and West Broadway.

"Read all about it! Crooked politicians in bribe scandal! Get your *New York World*, right here!"

Tommy's face lit up as he saw her approaching.

"There you are, Red! I've been waiting for you. Big news day. There's a scandal in City Hall. Good stuff. Here."

He gruffly handed her his bag of papers.

"Just follow me and watch a real salesman in action."

Free of the weight of the bag, Tommy snaked in and around the crowd much more easily and planted himself in front of potential customers. Each one got a different pitch.

"Dirty politicians are influencing the banking industry. Get the story right here," he said to a neatly dressed businessman.

To a middle-aged woman pushing a baby stroller, he said,

"There's a masher loose in Central Park attacking innocent women. Everything you need to know is in today's *World*!"

Sarah chased after him, collecting their pennies and making change for nickels and dimes.

Eventually, the pile of papers in the bag dwindled until the last one was sold. Tommy and Sarah sat on the stoop of a building and carefully counted out and divided their coins.

"Mr. Duffy'll be happy tonight," Tommy said. "I haven't sold my whole load in weeks."

"What about your parents?"

"I don't have any," he said.

Sarah's heartbeat quickened. "You don't?"

"I never knew my mom. She died giving birth to me right after they came over from Ireland. Then it was just my dad and me. He worked tending the machines at a printer's shop. But he got the flu a couple years back. Been on my own ever since."

"I lost my parents too," she said. It felt good to be sharing her story with someone who had gone through the same thing. "My mother died a few weeks ago."

"I'm real sorry," he said. "Who've you got looking out for you then?"

"For now, my uncle," she said. "But I'm going to have to find my own place to live soon. Do you know of anywhere?"

"Well, there are a few boardinghouses for boys that some of the newsies live in. But you need to pay five cents a night for rent. And they can be kinda rough. I don't think they have them for girls, 'cause there aren't really girl newsies."

"Oh," she said. "That's too bad."

"I wish I could let you stay with me and Mr. Duffy. But he's awfully strict and there's not much room anyway."

"Where do you live?"

"Oh, we've got a great little spot right near the corner of Bleecker and Wooster Street."

"Bleecker and Wooster? Where is that?"

"It's just a little uptown from here. Maybe we'll have you around for dinner sometime. You can be my date."

She laughed.

"What's the matter?" he said, crossing his arms. "You don't like shorter guys?"

"I would be happy to join you for dinner," she said.

"Do you have to ask your uncle?"

"My uncle?" Caught off guard, she stared at him, confused.

"Yeah."

"Oh! No, he wouldn't mind."

Suddenly, out of the corner of her eye, Sarah noticed someone staring at her from across the street—a short man with glasses in a brown uniform. He looked familiar, but she couldn't immediately place him. Then it came to her: Johnson, the guard from the Lady's island who had called Maryk a half-breed.

The breath instantly drained from her lungs.

"Hey," Tommy said, "what's wrong?"

Johnson held her gaze for another moment and then walked away.

Sarah's body unclenched, but her face was still filled with concern.

"Who was that?"

"Nobody," she said.

"I've never seen anyone get so spooked by 'nobody' before. Is there something you're not telling me?" His eyes narrowed with suspicion.

"No."

"Are you sure?"

More than anything, Sarah wanted to tell Tommy her whole story. But she didn't want to risk getting Maryk and Mrs. Lee in trouble, since she wasn't supposed to be here.

"No," she said. "Everything's fine."

"Okay. If you say so. Well, I gotta go," he said. "Mr. Duffy gets mad if I don't check in with him every couple of hours."

Tommy rose and hurried off uptown. As Sarah watched him go, she felt a chilling fear settle inside her. What was Johnson doing in Chinatown? Did he live there? It seemed unlikely. Could he have been spying on Maryk? Or maybe even looking for her?

A Strange Expression

Over the next several days, Sarah fell into a regular pattern of working with Mrs. Lee at mealtimes and then helping Tommy sell the morning and afternoon editions of the papers in between. With Sarah's help, Tommy was able to sell more, and she began to amass a sizable collection of pennies, which she kept hidden in a small cloth sack tucked deep under the mattress in Maryk's room, along with the coins she had collected on the island. Her sense of security grew with each coin. Soon she'd have enough money to rent her own room when Mrs. Lee made her leave.

She was cleaning the lunch dishes one afternoon when Mrs. Lee walked over to her.

"Maryk forgot the dinner I make. You go bring it to him."

She handed Sarah a small tin pot and a container of coffee.

"Where?"

"West side. Take Canal Street all the way over and then turn right. He work at Clews' Stable near the river."

"A stable?"

"Yes. Place to keep horses. He work there part-time."

Sarah knew what the word meant. Her stomach dropped.

"You go now," Mrs. Lee said. "Maryk get cranky if he not have food. But I guess Maryk get cranky if he have food too."

Sarah took the lunch and reluctantly set off to find the stable. She walked west several blocks until she arrived at a large fenced-in grassy area near the Hudson River filled with horses in various paddocks. Some of the horses trotted and grazed around a large open pasture.

Sarah circled the stable looking for Maryk and finally found him mucking out one of the pens with a metal rake. A large black mare grazed at the opposite end of the pen, which had a worn riding circle along the inside of its perimeter. Maryk's eyes narrowed as he caught sight of her.

"You forgot your meal," Sarah said, holding up the metal pot and coffee container.

"Thanks," Maryk grunted as he set the rake aside and approached.

He looked slightly annoyed, or maybe embarrassed that anyone was seeing him doing such lowly work.

Suddenly, the black mare whinnied loudly. Sarah recoiled and took a step back, dropping the metal pail. Half of Maryk's dinner spilled out into the mud.

"Hey!" Maryk said. "Watch what you're doing there."

"Sorry," Sarah said, scrambling to pick up the pail and salvage the portion of fried rice that had not hit the ground.

"Aw, just leave it!" Maryk barked.

"There is still some that is all right," she said, holding up the pail with the remaining food. She fearfully eyed the horse, which had moved closer to her, drawn by the smell of the food. She edged back.

"What's got you so spooked about horses anyway?"

She had a brief flash of the night her father died and the riderless horse barreling through their village.

"I just don't like them," Sarah replied.

"Put that stuff down and come here," he said.

Sarah placed the pail and container at her feet. Maryk stepped over to the black mare, which was already tacked up with a saddle and bridle, and grabbed the reins.

"Come on," he said. "I haven't got all day."

Sarah warily entered the pen and edged up to Maryk and the horse.

"Name's Betty," he said. "You're going to ride her."

"I can't," she said, shaking her head.

"Course you can," he said impatiently. "How you going to survive in New York if you're afraid of horses?"

"I can walk on my own feet," she said.

"I'm not expecting you to enter the Kentucky Derby or anything. Best thing to do is to face your fear head-on."

She stared at him doubtfully.

"Look, like I said, I haven't got all day." Maryk frowned. "So you're going to get on this horse right now and give this a try.

Animals smell fear. So I suggest you calm down. She ain't gonna bite you."

Sarah took a deep breath.

"Come on," he said. "First thing to remember is to always approach a horse from its left side."

Sarah inched toward the horse, staring into her large, dark eyes.

"Now put your hand on her neck and rub her shoulder," he commanded.

She tentatively reached out her hand and stroked the horse's neck, marveling at the smooth and hard muscle beneath. The horse whinnied softly.

"That's good. Now come around and give her a good look in the eye and then blow some breath into her nose."

"What?"

"Blow some of your breath into her nostrils. Animals learn about things by smelling them. It's kind of like a handshake."

Maryk's instructions were firm but clear. So Sarah faced the horse and then leaned in and blew into her nose. The horse shook her head calmly.

"Here." He reached into his pocket and extracted a carrot. "Give her this. Best way to make friends with anyone, man or beast, is to offer them something to eat. Go on."

Sarah took the carrot and cautiously held it up toward the horse's mouth.

She flinched as the animal leaned in and snatched the carrot with her huge yellow teeth. Her body tingled.

"Okay, now take the reins right there. Hold them tight, but don't pull them. Then grab the saddle with your other hand. Put your left foot into that stirrup and kind of push yourself up."

Sarah took a deep breath and attempted to mount. Her right leg grazed the horse's back, causing the animal to shuffle. Sarah flailed, lost her balance, and fell.

"Ow!" she grunted as she hit the ground. Sharp pain spread from her tailbone up her back.

"You almost had it," he said. "Give yourself more of a push up with that left leg."

Sarah stood up, dusted herself off, and again grabbled the reins and put her left foot into the stirrup. She gritted her teeth, flexed her muscles, and hauled herself up onto the horse.

"That's it," he said. "Now balance yourself."

Sarah wobbled and gripped the saddle for dear life.

"Just relax," Maryk said. "Don't forget to breathe."

Sarah took a deep breath, straightened her back, and paused a moment to admire her surroundings from the unfamiliar height. The city spread out before her to her left; the majestic river rolled by on her right. For the first time she was able to see that Maryk had a small bald patch at the crown of his otherwise thick head of hair.

"Okay, now just squeeze your legs together. That should get her going."

Sarah gently applied pressure with her legs to the horse's sides, and the animal instantly moved forward. Jarred off balance, Sarah almost slipped, but she held on. The powerful muscles of the mare flexed beneath her and she started to move around the riding circle. Slowly, Sarah relaxed and got into sync with the rhythm of the horse's motion.

"That's it," Maryk said. "Now just pull the reins the way you want to turn."

Sarah did as instructed and guided the horse around the circle.

As the animal picked up speed, the breeze from the river blew back Sarah's hair. She saw flashes of the blue sky, clouds, sun, and the other horses and buildings whir past.

She rode for several minutes, until she finally noticed Maryk leaning against the fence watching her. He wore a strange expression on his face, and at first she thought he was grimacing in pain. She didn't want to stare, so she sneaked quick glances as she rode in the circle. It took a few turns around the ring for Sarah to realize that Maryk was actually smiling. She had never seen his face bent into such an unnatural position. And she felt an unexpected rush of warmth at having pleased him.

Another America

AFTER HER RIDE, SARAH HELPED Maryk finish mucking out the horse pens, and then they walked to Mrs. Lee's together in the gathering twilight.

"Thank you," she said.

"It was nothing," he grunted. "Hold on a minute."

He paused and removed his pipe and tobacco pouch from his jacket. As he did, something fell from the pocket and fluttered to the ground.

Sarah bent to pick it up. It was the photograph of the woman and the baby, the one she had found hidden in the chess set. She held it out toward him, but he nodded at her, wordlessly giving her permission to look at it.

She carefully examined the image of the young mother and child. The woman had thick, dark hair parted in the middle and arranged in an elaborate braid that hung over her shoulder. She wore a white dress with simple embroidered flowers around the neckline. She had a shy expression on her face, and almost seemed to be turning away from the camera. The baby sat in her lap and wore a ribbon in her hair with a lace-trimmed nightgown.

"Beautiful," Sarah said. "Both beautiful."

"Yeah." He nodded solemnly. "She would've been about your age by now."

He took the photo from her and put it back in his pocket, and then put his pipe and tobacco away without lighting up.

"Come on," he said. "Let's go."

They continued walking together. Maryk's eyes were fixed in the distance, as if he were lost in his memories. Sarah yearned to know more about his secret past.

"What happened to them?"

Maryk cleared his throat.

"The pox got them," he said without breaking stride.

"What is that?"

"A bad sickness. Some people die from it. Some don't. Some don't have to."

"I don't understand."

"There're ways to treat the pox. Doctors have medicines that can stop it."

"Medicines didn't work for them?"

"It wasn't the medicine. It was the damn doctor who didn't work."

"I do not understand."

He sighed and took in another deep breath but never stopped walking, his eyes fixed in the distance.

"I was a horseman like my father. Working for a traveling circus going from state to state. We were in the middle of the country in a small town. The baby got sick first, fever so high I thought she was going to fry in her own skin. I took her to see the local doctor. It was the middle of the night, so I had to rouse him out of bed. But he took one look at my child and my wife and wouldn't treat her. Said he didn't want to risk infection for a dark baby."

"Dark?"

"Dark-skinned. My wife was Mexican. Our child looked like a cross between her and my Indian mother." His face took on a serene expression as he described her. "So her skin was reddish brown. Like the color of coffee, milk, and cinnamon all mixed together."

Maryk's face darkened as he continued.

"Anyway, when he refused to treat her, I took a horse from the circus's stable and rode thirty miles with both of them to a reservation of the Pawnee tribe. My mother's people were Dakota, but it didn't matter to them. They took us in and the tribe's healer did what he could, but by then it was too late to save her. Soon after that, it was clear that my wife had the pox too."

He lapsed into a heavy silence.

"What were their names?"

"My wife was Maria-Elena. And the baby's name was Daisy. Daisy Raye."

"They are nice names."

"This country has a lot of good to it. But there's another America out there that's not so pretty. They don't write poems about that America and put them on postcards of the Statue of Liberty."

Sarah thought about what Smitty had said about people not wanting to hire him because of his skin color. When Sarah and her mother had dreamed of the promised land, it had never occurred to them that Americans were so different from each other and weren't all treated equally.

"My father and I were the only redheads in our village. The other children used to make fun of me and call me Carrot Head and other stupid names. My father said that we were special and that we were the last of the family redheads and should be proud of it. But it wasn't easy to do that when I was little. I really am the last one now."

Maryk grunted and nodded. Sarah fell silent for a moment, as the full truth of the words sank in.

"He also told me that God doesn't pay attention to hair color, so people shouldn't either."

"Sounds like he was a very wise man."

"He was." Sarah nodded.

Talking about her father made Sarah feel sad, but it also brought back some warm memories, and sharing them made her feel closer to Maryk.

"Do you have any other family?" she asked.

"My mother had a brother and he had a couple of kids—my cousins. Jim and Wayne. They live out on reservation land some-where near Oklahoma City."

"What is reservation land?"

"A place they put all the Indians, keep 'em in one place so they don't cause trouble except to themselves."

His voice was tinged with bitterness, and he looked away as if he was ashamed to be even talking about it.

"Do you see them?"

"Naw, I haven't been back there in years. Decades."

"Why?"

"Guess I've been trying to stay as far away from the past as I can. We send each other postcards at the holidays. That's about it. I know they've got families of their own. They're good people but . . . they've got their lives, and I've got mine."

"Why did you come to the city?"

Maryk looked up at the buildings and people rushing around them.

"New York is a good place to disappear. I found a part-time job as a horse trainer at the stable. But there wasn't enough work there to keep me fed, so I started working as a night watchman on the island. At least I did until now."

"What do you mean?"

He coughed and cleared his throat.

"I got suspended from the job."

"What is suspended?"

"That means I can't go to work for a while."

"Why?"

"For having an unauthorized visitor during my shift."

"Unauthorized?"

"That means someone who wasn't supposed to be there."

Sarah's throat went dry.

"Me?"

Maryk nodded.

"You remember Johnson? The little guy with the glasses?"

"Yes," she said, feeling the blood in her veins run cold.

"He's always had it out for me," Maryk said. "Doesn't like my kind."

Sarah wondered if she should tell Maryk that she had seen Johnson in Chinatown, but she held her tongue, not wanting to upset him further.

"He must've told my boss as soon as he saw you in the guard-house."

"I'm sorry. I will go and explain—"

"No."

"I can't let you lose your job because of me. . . ."

"I haven't been fired yet. There's going to be an investigation."

"An investigation?"

"That just means they're going to look into my work record, ask people questions about me. That kind of thing."

"I should leave here. You'll get in trouble if they find me."

"They don't know anything about you. This is about me. And they won't come here looking. I just have to sober up for a while and tuck in my shirt when I go talk to my supervisor. That kind of thing. Don't worry. I've been suspended before. I've just got to lay off the booze and turn on the charm, not that I have any left to turn on."

"What does that mean, 'turn on the charm'?"

"It means that I've got to start acting like a human being again, instead of a mean old drunkard."

"Drunkard?"

"Yeah."

She stared at him, still not quite comprehending.

"That's someone who drinks too much and acts like an animal. Like me."

They walked on in silence.

Bao Yu

BACK AT MRS. LEE'S, MARYK WENT to the basement to rest. Sarah retreated upstairs, her head filled with concerns about all he had shared with her. Moving down the hall toward her room, Sarah was surprised to find Bao Yu standing by the door, waiting for her.

"Hello," Sarah said.

"Hi," Bao Yu replied. She spoke in a low voice, almost as if she was embarrassed to be speaking at all. "May I talk to you for a minute?"

"Yes," Sarah said. "Come in."

She ushered Bao Yu into Maryk's room and closed the door behind them.

Bao Yu stood in a spot just inside the door and tentatively looked around.

"My mother would not want me to be here," she said. "She is taking a nap now."

"She doesn't like me very much," Sarah said.

"It's not you. It's me. She does not want me to mix with anyone."

"Why not?"

"She hopes to find me a Chinese boy to marry from a good family, who will want a traditional girl. She doesn't want me to become too American."

"She thinks I am too American?" Sarah almost laughed.

"No, but you are not Chinese. Chinese boys want to marry girls who know the old ways, who have not become too modern."

Sarah giggled. How could anyone think of her as "modern"?

"She wants you to get married now?" Sarah said. "Aren't you my age?"

"I just turned twelve."

"Isn't that too young to get married?"

"Maybe not married, but my mother believes it's never too early to find a match. My mother was promised to my father when she was half my age. Marriage came later, but the families made the arrangements long in advance. She's hoping to make a match as soon as possible."

"That happened in my old country too," Sarah said, excited to be sharing something of her past. "There were matchmakers who put boys and girls together. My friends and I used to worry about who the matchmaker would pair us with and pray it wasn't one of the ugly boys. There was one boy named Abram who had greasy hair and smelled like sour milk." She winced at the memory.

"Yuck," Bao Yu said, wrinkling her nose.

"All the girls called him Milk Boy behind his back," Sarah said.

Both girls laughed. Then Bao Yu's smile disappeared and her brow furrowed.

"I have come to ask a favor," she said.

"A favor?" Sarah said, wondering what anyone could want from her.

"I've seen you reading the newspaper. And even some of these books." She gestured to Maryk's bookshelf. "Do you think you could teach me?"

"Your mother and father never taught you?"

"My mother doesn't know how to read either. She never went to school."

"Mine didn't either," Sarah said, feeling good that they shared something else in common.

"She took care of her parents and then she took care of me and my father. That was her job. But I need to learn if I'm ever going to help support my mother."

"I suppose I could try," Sarah said, flattered to be asked.

"I don't have any money to pay you."

"Don't worry about that. It'll be nice for me just to have someone to talk to besides Mrs. Lee and Miss Jean."

"But it would have to be our secret. My mother would be furious if she ever found out."

"Of course," Sarah said. "We can meet in the afternoons when your mother takes her nap."

"That would be wonderful," Bao Yu said.

"Can I ask you a question?" Sarah said.

"Of course."

"What does the name Bao Yu mean?"

"It's Cantonese," she said. "It means 'precious jade.'"

"That's pretty," Sarah said. "Those will be some of the first words I'll need to teach you."

"Thank you," Bao Yu said.

She reached into her pocket and handed Sarah something in a small white wrapper.

"It's ginger candy."

Bao Yu bowed slightly and then quietly slipped out of the room.

Sarah unwrapped the candy and put it in her mouth. It was soft and sweet and slightly spicy and got stuck in her teeth as she chewed.

The Conversation

THAT NIGHT, SARAH GOT out of bed to use the toilet down the hall. Her thighs and calves ached from horseback riding as she squatted down on the cold wooden seat.

The house was dark and quiet as she made her way back to her room in her stocking feet. But she paused when she heard voices and noticed a dim light coming from downstairs. She wondered who could be up at that hour, so she tiptoed over to the stairs, leaned her head down, and listened.

The muffled voices of Maryk and Mrs. Lee drifted up from the kitchen. She couldn't make out what they were saying. So she carefully moved down to the bottom of the stairs until she could clearly hear their voices and the low rattle of glasses on the wood kitchen table.

"You drink too much of that stuff," Mrs. Lee said. "Makes your stomach sour and eyes red."

"You saying you don't want any?"

"Just a little," she said.

"I figured as much."

"I have nip in tea. You drink whole bottle. Not the same."

"Everybody's got their poison."

Sarah heard the sound of whiskey being poured. And then a long silence.

"So what you going to do with her?" Mrs. Lee finally said.

"What do you mean, what am I gonna do?"

"I mean, what you going to do with the girl?"

"It's not just me now. You're in this too."

"You get me in. I don't want to be in. With Sarah here along with Chinese girls, people get wrong ideas, think I run slave ring. I could go to jail. I could lose everything."

"No one's even noticed."

"Not true. Mr. Wong next door ask who she is."

"What'd you say?"

"I said she was your niece like we decide."

"Did he believe you?"

"I think. Don't know."

"Hmm," Maryk grunted. "Well, Wong always has been a nosy son of a gun."

"Not just Mr. Wong notice. Others too."

"Who?"

"Lots others. Mrs. Fat not happy. She want job for Bao Yu."

"Fat's never happy."

"I told you she could stay for one week."

"You want to throw her out on the street? Is that what you want?"

Another long silence followed. Sarah held her breath, waiting for the reply.

"She a good girl," Mrs. Lee said softly.

"You think I don't know that?"

"So what *we* going to do with her?"

"I just don't know."

Another silence. Mrs. Lee sighed.

"I need to sleep," she finally said.

Sarah heard Mrs. Lee rise from the table. She quickly stepped back and felt the blood rush into her head. After gripping the railing to steady herself, she tiptoed up the stairs to Maryk's room and locked the door.

She got back into the bed, covered herself under the warm blankets, and propped Ivan on the pillow beside her.

"I've got to think of something to do so she'll have to let me stay."

The toy bear looked back at her blankly.

"You're not any help. I don't know why I bother talking to you."

She sighed, lay back, and stared at the ceiling. There was only one thing she could think to do.

Spotless

BY FIVE THIRTY A.M. SARAH'S KNEES were raw. But she continued scrubbing the kitchen floor in the semidarkness. She had been cleaning for well over an hour, first straightening the front room, then setting the dining table for the morning meal, and finally landing in the kitchen to prepare breakfast and make the place as spotless as possible.

She was working a rough-bristled brush over and over a dark stain near the sink when Mrs. Lee entered and watched her in silence for a moment.

"That stain older than Mrs. Lee," she said.

Sarah jumped. "You surprised me," she said, rising to her feet.

"You surprised me too," Mrs. Lee said.

"I was just cleaning."

"I see. Parlor swept. Dining table set."

"I can get up early and do the work, so you can sleep more."

"You think Mrs. Lee so old she need more sleep?"

"No. I was just . . ."

"It was joke," Mrs. Lee said.

"And I have some money," Sarah said. She gestured to the kitchen table, where she had laid out the coins she'd collected on the Lady's island and working for Tommy. "It's not much," she continued, "but I can make more and pay for a room."

"Come here and sit," Mrs. Lee said, with a gentler voice than Sarah was used to hearing.

Sarah placed her brush in the sink and sat at the kitchen table.

"You good worker."

"Thank you."

"You like it here?"

Sarah nodded.

"I make decision."

"A decision?"

"Yes. I decide you can stay."

Mrs. Lee patted Sarah's hand, crossed her arms, and nodded.

A lump formed in Sarah's throat.

"I can stay?"

"Yes, and work for me. You okay with working for mean old Chinese lady?"

"You aren't mean," Sarah said.

"So you do think I am old." Mrs. Lee's eyes went wide in mock anger.

"No . . . I . . . thank you."

Sarah rose from her chair and hugged Mrs. Lee.

Mrs. Lee's face softened and she gave Sarah a pat on the back.

"And you keep your money," she said, nodding to the coins. "You will earn your keep working for me. It is full-time job. No more wandering around. Don't want people asking questions either. You understand?"

Sarah wouldn't be able to help Tommy sell his papers anymore. As happy as she was about Mrs. Lee's decision, she dreaded telling Tommy that she would have to put their business partnership on hold.

"Yes," she said. "I understand."

Sarah retreated upstairs to Maryk's room, closed the door, and jumped onto the bed. She squeezed the pillow tightly, a rush of joy and relief washing over her. She had a home. It wasn't like any home she had ever imagined having, but it was enough to know she would have a roof over her head and be safe and welcome somewhere.

Losses

SARAH STAYED INSIDE NEARLY all the next day. It was only when the sun had started to set that Mrs. Lee finally let her go out to buy the evening papers. Sarah nervously fingered the coins in her pocket as she wound her way down Mott Street, looking for Tommy.

She found him standing on the corner, calling out headlines with a heavy bag of evening papers weighing down his shoulder. She approached, dreading having to break the news.

"Where you been, Red?" he said. "I've been looking all over for you."

He unslung the bag from his shoulder and placed it at his feet, so she could take it up.

"Sorry, I—"

"I didn't sell near as many of the morning paper as we did yesterday," he interrupted. "But come on, let's see if we can unload these quick."

Sarah took a deep breath.

"Tommy, I can't sell papers with you anymore."

"What? But I thought we were partners. I thought you needed to save money to get your own place."

"I did," she said. "But now I will be able to stay with my uncle for a while. And the woman who runs the house wants me to work for her full-time."

His face fell. "Oh," he said.

"I am sorry."

"It's okay. I'm happy for you. It's just that I told Mr. Duffy all about our partnership. He thought it was a good idea."

"Will Mr. Duffy be mad?"

"Oh, no. He's a swell guy. He never gets mad at me."

"Are you sure?" she said.

"Sure I'm sure," Tommy said, forcing a smile. "Don't worry about me. Everyone knows Tommy Grogan's the best newsie in Manhattan. I just got to work on building up my muscles."

He flexed his small biceps.

"I promise I'll always buy from you," Sarah said. "And I'll take three now."

She paid him and he handed her the papers.

"Thanks," he said, hoisting the bag back on his shoulder. "Well, I'd better get a move on. Only a little more daylight to sell my stack."

"Are you sure you're all right?"

"Sure," he said. "Don't worry about me, Sarah."

It was the first time Tommy had ever used her real name. Something about the way he said it, with all of his usual bravado stripped away, made her worry about him even more.

"See you around," he said.

Tommy moved off through the crowd, waving a paper in the air.

"Get your *New York World* here! All the dirt! Read all about it!"

Sarah watched him wander away and then headed back to the apartment building.

As she walked, Sarah glanced into shop windows until she froze at the sight of someone who looked familiar inside a small, dingy jewelry store. She moved closer and realized that it was Mrs. Fat, talking to the man behind the counter. At first, Sarah thought it was strange that Mrs. Fat would be jewelry shopping. Then she realized that the jeweler was holding a jade bracelet in his hand and examining it with a magnifying glass while Mrs. Fat talked.

Finally, the jeweler looked up and offered her a few dollars from a cashbox. Mrs. Fat threw up her hands, as if insulted by the offer. The jeweler shrugged and placed the money in the box and the bracelet back on the counter. Mrs. Fat didn't take the bracelet. She continued pleading with him, but he just shook his head. Finally she sighed and nodded. He produced the same measly collection of bills and handed them to Mrs. Fat.

As she counted the bills, Mrs. Fat glanced up and looked out the window.

Sarah quickly joined the flow of people moving down the sidewalk and hurried away. She thought of Bao Yu's name, "precious jade," and realized how difficult it must have been for Mrs. Fat to part with the bracelet.

When Sarah returned to the building, Miss Jean had just finished pulling the dried laundry from the line in the backyard. Sarah helped her fold the sheets and towels and then delivered the laundered linens to all the boarders.

Sarah made her delivery rounds and saved Mrs. Fat and Bao Yu's room for last, afraid of seeing the woman. She gently knocked on the door, holding their neatly folded pile of white sheets.

"Bao Yu, get the door," she heard Mrs. Fat say from inside. Her voice sounded muffled and strange.

After a moment Bao Yu opened the door.

"I have your laundry," Sarah said.

Sarah peered into the apartment and could see Mrs. Fat was on her knees crying before what appeared to be a small altar. At the center of the altar was a framed photograph of a Chinese man in a dark suit, surrounded by a ceramic bowl containing an orange; a statue of a fat, bald man sitting cross-legged; and two red candles.

Mrs. Fat caught sight of Sarah and wiped her eyes.

"Get out," she said.

Sarah looked away.

Bao Yu took the pile of laundry from Sarah. Their eyes met. Sarah could see Bao Yu fighting back tears as she gently closed the door.

English Lessons

OVER THE NEXT FEW days, Sarah managed to find time in the afternoon to work with Bao Yu on her English. She never mentioned seeing Mrs. Fat selling the bracelet.

At first Sarah started with the basic alphabet and then worked her way up to simple words. For reading lessons she used Maryk's book of Aesop's fables, and for writing instruction, she made Bao Yu copy sentences from old newspapers. Since they had no paper to work with, Sarah had her copy the words into the margins of the newspapers themselves, until every inch of blank space was covered with densely packed words.

Sarah tried to make the lessons fun. She would dictate silly rhyming sentences that would be easy for Bao Yu to spell.

"The rat sat on the hat," Sarah said.

"Why would he sit on a hat?" Bao Yu said. "Wouldn't he wear it?"

"Rats don't wear hats," Sarah said. "And I haven't taught you how to spell the word *wear* yet. Just write what I tell you."

"The rat sat on the hat . . . ," Bao Yu said, as she wrote.

"Then he was bit by the cat," Sarah continued. "And they were both hit with a bat."

"And it made them flat?" Bao Yu added.

"Splat," Sarah said, nodding. Both girls giggled.

Suddenly, there was a knock at the door and both girls fell silent and looked at each other. Sarah mouthed the words, "Your mother?" Bao Yu shrugged. Another knock.

"You going to open door?" Mrs. Lee's voice called. "Or make me stand in hall all day?"

The girls quickly hid their writing lesson beneath the mattress, and Sarah opened the door. Mrs. Lee entered carrying a small paper bag.

"About time," she said impatiently.

"Sorry," Sarah said.

"I know what you do in here," she said.

"What do you mean? We aren't doing anything wrong," Sarah said nervously. Bao Yu stared down at her feet.

"Didn't say you did something wrong," Mrs. Lee said. "But it my house. I know what go on. Find newspapers covered with letters and words in trash every day."

"I only used old papers," Sarah started to explain. "Once I knew everyone had already read them."

"I know," Mrs. Lee said. "I brought you this. To share."

Mrs. Lee handed Sarah the bag; inside were two small lined notebooks and two brand-new pencils.

"You can use to practice," Mrs. Lee said.

Sarah and Bao Yu each stared in awe at the gift. Neither girl was used to receiving presents.

"Thank you, Mrs. Lee," Bao Yu said.

"Thank you very much," Sarah said.

"You will not tell my mother?" Bao Yu said.

Mrs. Lee looked at her and shook her head.

"It is good thing when girls help other girls. Sometime the only way girls can survive is when they help each other. You keep going with lesson now. Sarah, you still have half hour before we start dinner."

Mrs. Lee abruptly turned and exited.

Run!

"CHECKMATE," MARYK SAID, SLAPPING the table with delight as he captured her king.

Sarah stared at the board in disbelief, trying to figure out what she had done wrong.

For several days she had been playing chess with Maryk and the other boarders during her free time. And until that moment no one had been able to beat her. But Maryk's game had improved significantly with each day, and now he finally had his first victory.

He rose from the chair and did a little dance with her captured king and queen. "Told you I was just a little rusty."

"Let's play again," she said, quickly resetting her pieces.

"Oh no," he said, sitting back down with a satisfied grin. "I want to savor this win for at least a day before I give you another chance to make me look like a fool. You should always remember that when you beat someone at something, you want to give them a little time to marinate in the defeat so it really sticks to 'em."

"What is marinate?"

"When you soak something in a liquid so it picks up the flavor. Next time we play, I want you to still have the taste of losing on you."

"I will be sure to take a bath tonight."

"I feel like celebrating my victory. Why don't you run around the corner to Kang's shop and buy me some fresh tobacco. Buy yourself a sweet, too. I'm feeling generous."

He handed her a nickel.

"I like Kenwood brand pipe tobacco," he said. "Comes in a green tin. Should be three cents. That'll leave you two cents for some sweets. Go on."

Sarah went down the block to Kang's Corner, a dry goods store that sold tobacco, candy, and other small household items. Kang, the proprietor, was a heavyset man who stood behind the shop's counter wearing a white coat that buttoned from his collar to his knees.

She found Maryk's tobacco and then took her time picking out her candy, which was displayed on shelves behind the counter. There were dozens of glass jars filled with lollipops and candy canes of all colors and stripes, chocolate taffy, candied fruit wedges, gumdrops, and licorice whips.

She finally settled on a selection of grape, apple, mint, and cherry candy canes. They would give her the most flavor for her money.

She handed Kang the nickel and he deposited everything into a paper sack.

On the way back to the apartment, Sarah unwrapped one of the candy canes. She closed her eyes with pleasure as she took her first lick of the grape-flavored treat. If she licked carefully, she could make it last for hours.

As she rounded the corner onto her street, Sarah stopped short when she saw a group of men gathered outside the front entrance of Mrs. Lee's building. Terror ran through her as she realized that none of these men were Chinese. They all wore sharp blue uniforms with black leather belts with brass buckles. Polished dark wood nightsticks hung at their sides.

Her mind froze.

Are they here for me?

The front door of the house opened and more men in uniform led out the four Chinese girls. The girls looked helpless and confused as they were ushered to a large horse-drawn wagon that waited on the street. One of the men opened the back door of the wagon, which had a small window crisscrossed with iron bars, and pushed the first girl inside. Next, Mrs. Lee emerged, with another tall man in uniform pulling her by the arm.

"You make mistake," Mrs. Lee said. "Everything legal here!"

"Tell it to the judge," the policeman said.

He maneuvered her toward the other girls, who were being loaded into the back of the wagon.

Finally, Maryk emerged from the building, led out by two police officers, one on each side. Squinting into the sunlight, Maryk paused at the doorway.

He looked out onto the street and his eyes found Sarah. They stared at each other for a moment, his face filled with concern. Then he quickly shook his head.

He wanted her to stay away.

Just then, Sarah saw Johnson emerge from behind the police wagon, watching the raid, wearing a satisfied smirk. His small, spectacled eyes followed the direction of Maryk's glance and caught sight of Sarah.

"That girl is one of them!" he shouted.

Sarah's eyes widened with fear.

"Run!" Maryk mouthed.

A Small Tugging

"HEY, YOU! HOLD IT RIGHT THERE!"

Sarah dropped the paper bag she was holding and took off toward Mott Street. She glanced over her shoulder. Two of the police officers were running after her.

"Someone stop that girl!" one yelled.

She almost gagged as the grape candy momentarily got stuck in the back of her throat. She pulled it out of her mouth and threw it to the ground.

The Chinese men on the street looked up as Sarah sped by them, followed by the lumbering policemen. Because of her size, Sarah had an easier time navigating through the sea of bodies than the men, who took out their nightsticks and used them to prod people out of the way.

"Move it!" she heard them growl. "C'mon. Out of my way!"

Sarah ran north until she came to Canal Street, a busy thoroughfare clogged with carriages, horses, and people moving across town in both directions. As she darted into the traffic, she nearly collided with a fast-trotting horse-drawn carriage. She cut in front of the horse, her shoulder grazing the animal as she passed. The horse reared up and whinnied loudly, causing Sarah to trip and fall in the middle of the street.

The enormous animal rocked back on its muscular hind legs and raised its front hooves, ready to trample her. Sarah closed her eyes tightly, held her breath, and waited for the deathblow. But the carriage driver yanked on the reins and pulled the horse to the left. The animal's hooves crashed down beside Sarah's head and the carriage continued down the street.

Sarah opened her eyes and looked back. The policemen were right behind her now, just a few yards away.

"Stop that girl!"

She felt sure they would catch her and considered just giving herself up.

Just then, an old bearded man with a pushcart piled high with multicolored rags stepped into the path of the policemen, momentarily blocking their progress.

"Hey!" the policemen yelled at the old man. "Move this thing!"

Seizing the opportunity, Sarah sprang to her feet and sprinted across Canal. She ran a few blocks north, having no idea where she was heading or where she should go. She turned right down a smaller side street, then took an immediate left down another.

Finally, she was able to duck into an alley and hide behind a half dozen wooden barrels with rusted metal lids. Laundry lines filled with drying clothes zigzagged up over her head between the two buildings that formed the alley, filtering the waning sunlight into jagged yellow flares.

She fought to quiet her breathing as she peered out from behind the barrels and stared into the street. After just a few seconds, her body tensed as she saw the two policemen enter her field of vision. She pulled herself back behind the barrels as one of them stepped into the mouth of the alley. Sarah held her breath, willing herself to be as still and silent as possible.

The policeman took his nightstick and slammed it on top of the first barrel with a loud clang. Sarah flinched.

"All right, come out!" he said. "I know you're in there."

Clang! Clang! He slammed his stick on the barrel again and then waited in the echo. Sarah bit her bottom lip and stifled a cry of fear.

Clang!

Another beat of silence.

"She ain't in here," he called to his partner. "You see her out there?"

"No," the other called. "She must have cut down Kenmare."

"Great," the first policeman said. "My feet are killing me."

He reattached the nightstick to his belt and ambled after his partner.

Sarah remained still for a long time, making sure they weren't setting a trap for her. Finally, she peered out from behind the barrel. The alley was empty and the sky was darkening so the street disappeared under a veil of gray.

Unlike Mott, this street wasn't crowded with as many pedestrians. And most of the people she saw were not Chinese. She heard snippets of English and Italian being spoken, and even some Yiddish. She decided she wouldn't venture out into the street again until night had fallen.

Sarah huddled behind the barrels for another two hours as the air grew colder and a chill settled into her skin and penetrated her bones. The same questions kept rattling through her mind. Why were the police there? Had Smitty and Miss Jean been arrested too? And what about Bao Yu and Mrs. Fat? Maybe they had all been arrested because of her.

No matter the cause, she knew she could not go back there. Her empty stomach twisted at the thought of her new friends in jeopardy. But the more pressing question was, where would she go now?

Just then Sarah felt a small tugging on the back of her coat, and she craned her neck over her shoulder to see what it was. A fat black rat was nibbling on the hem of her garment.

Sarah screamed and jerked up. But the rat hung on, its sharp yellow teeth sunk into the fabric.

Night on the Bowery

SARAH JUMPED UP AND down, but the rat just dug its claws in and began to climb up her back. Her skin crawled as the animal inched higher and higher, until she could feel it touching the edge of her hair. She whipped off her coat and swung it against the wall of a building. Finally, the rat fell free and scurried away. Sarah bolted out of the alley as fast as she could.

She ran past vendors closing up for the night, stalls that sold tomatoes and big jugs of olive oil, and stores with huge sausages and cheeses on strings hanging in the windows. There were no Chinese people to be seen. Everyone seemed to be speaking a different language. She had heard Mrs. Lee and Miss Jean mention an area of the city called Little Italy but hadn't known that it was so close by.

Sarah finally allowed herself to slow down to a fast walk, trying to put more distance between herself and the police who had been searching for her. She kept her eyes open for stray pieces of food and potential hiding places, but there were none. She passed several newsboys, trying to unload their last papers.

"Please, I've got to eat tonight," one said.

So do I, she thought.

She suddenly felt desperately hungry and cursed herself for dropping the candy when she ran. Sarah also wished she had the bag of coins she had earned with Tommy, but it was still buried beneath Maryk's mattress.

She came to another wide cross street lined with shops with more foot and horse traffic. A massive elevated train track ran up and down the street, casting everything below in deep, dark shadows. The wind howled and she pulled her coat tighter around herself. All the shops in this area were closed, but many dingy taverns were open. Groups of men huddled around the entrances to the bars, smoking cigars and talking and laughing with rough voices.

She cast her eyes down and kept moving. Past the dim lights of the taverns, the sidewalks were even darker and she saw other broken men sitting on the sidewalks in grimy heaps with their backs up against darkened buildings, drinking out of bottles and mumbling to themselves.

A loud clap of thunder shook the ground as a heavy rain started to fall from the dark sky. Sarah looked down every alley, searching for cover or a place to camp for the night, yet every dry spot was already taken by a bum or a newsie. And she suspected that these streets were too dangerous for her to sleep outside.

Where would she go? Who would take her in? Her relatives in

Brooklyn were gone. Maryk and Mrs. Lee had been taken away by the police. At least in the crown room of the Lady she had been protected from the elements. But there was no way to get back there at night.

Passing yet another tavern, she heard a rowdy crowd inside singing along to an out-of-tune piano. Snippets of the lyrics appeared to be warnings.

> *I struck a place that they called a "dive,"*
> *I was in luck to get out alive. . . .*
>
> *The Bow'ry! The Bow'ry!*
> *They say such things,*
> *And they do strange things*
> *On the Bow'ry! The Bow'ry!*
> *I'll never go there anymore!*

Despite the romping melody of the song, something about it sounded menacing to Sarah. Every voice seemed thickened with drink. Yet she knew she had to take cover, so she steeled herself and ducked inside.

The Egg

THE AIR IN THE ROOM WAS SO clouded with cigar smoke that she could barely see more than a few feet in front of her. Dozens of men crowded around the bar, holding mugs of beer or gathered around the piano that was against the back wall. There were just a few women in the room, and most of them wore low-cut dresses and had their hair hanging loose.

Sarah pressed herself into a shadowy corner, hoping to wait out the storm and not be noticed. A half-empty mug of beer sat on a counter nearby. Her throat constricted from thirst. The mug appeared to be abandoned, and she watched it closely to make sure no one would claim it.

Finally, she moved forward to grab the mug, but a man in a brown tattered coat and hat stepped into her path.

"Hey, girlie, can I buy you a drink?"

"No thank you," she said, shrinking back, hoping to become invisible again. But the man followed her back to her corner.

"Aw, come on," he said. "I won't bite."

Another man approached.

"Jimmy ain't got the teeth to do much damage anyway," he said.

The first man smiled and revealed a red, toothless upper gum.

Sarah recoiled. The men laughed.

"I just came in to find my father," she said.

"Your pa's here?"

"My mother told me to come fetch him for dinner. He's a police officer. Have you seen him?"

"A copper, you say?"

The men instinctively took a step back.

"Yes. A big man, with red hair."

"I haven't seen him. Have you seen him, Jimmy?"

"Naw, I haven't seen him neither."

"I'm going to look for him."

Sarah slipped between the two men and wound her way through the crowd to the other side of the bar, where she hid in the opposite corner.

Her mouth felt dry and her stomach ached with hunger. She spied a large jar of hard-boiled eggs, sitting on the wooden counter behind the bar. Dozens of white eggs floated in a clear yellowish liquid. Periodically the bartender would reach in and hand one out along with the drinks he served. Sarah's stomach groaned at the sight of the food.

The bartender placed one egg in front of a man sipping a large frothy mug of beer. The man left the egg untouched on the bar as he turned to talk to another man.

Sarah's eyes fixed on the egg, like an animal stalking its prey, waiting for an opportunity to pounce. She had scavenged piles of food on the Lady's island, but all of it had been thrown away or abandoned. If she took the egg, she knew, she would be crossing a different line, that she would be stealing food that was not hers. But she had to eat something.

Would anyone really care about a single egg?

It was not even clear to Sarah if the eggs cost any money. Maybe no one would notice or mind if she took it.

After a minute of observing the man and the egg, Sarah decided to make her move. She inched toward the bar, trying to simultaneously keep an eye on the bartender and the man drinking the beer. Saliva formed beneath her tongue in anticipation. She squeezed between a group of men crowded near the bar and slowly extended her arm.

A man accidentally jostled her and she pulled back for a moment. But then she carefully reached out her hand and grabbed the egg.

"What's this then?" the man with the frothy mug of beer said, as he caught sight of Sarah.

The bartender turned to look at her.

"The kid grabbed your egg, Charlie," another man said.

"What are you doing there, girl?" the man with the beer said.

Sarah's eyes widened in fear, but she did not let go of the egg.

"Get out of here, you little thief!" the bartender shouted as he made a move toward her.

Sarah quickly turned, snaked her way between men, and bolted back out into the rainy night.

No one seemed to be following her, but she ran on anyway. She shoved the egg into her mouth and was shocked by the briny, pickled flavor, completely unlike any egg she had ever eaten. She almost choked as she attempted to run, chew, and swallow at the same time. The yolk of the strange-tasting egg stuck in her throat, and one single, awful word the bartender had said echoed in her mind.

Thief.

A powerful sense of shame washed over her as she realized what she had become. From her earliest childhood, she had been taught that stealing was wrong, that it was one of the most important of the Ten Commandments delivered by God to Moses on Mount Sinai. She had never felt that she was doing anything wrong on the Lady's island, but now she was clearly guilty of something.

Those thoughts weighed on her almost as heavily as the question of where she would spend the night.

Bleecker Street

THE RAIN STARTED TO fall harder in thick sheets. She kept moving uptown, but within minutes she was completely drenched.

Reading street signs as she went, she walked by several drunks lying on the sidewalk, pulling long draws from their bottles, oblivious to the storm. Spring Street, Prince Street, Houston. The names had no meaning, but she read them anyway. Until she reached Bleecker Street and the name triggered something.

Bleecker Street.

That was where Tommy said he lived with Mr. Duffy! A spark of hope flickered inside her. Maybe if she could find them, they would let her stay for the night.

Tommy had said he lived on the corner of Bleecker and another street, but she couldn't remember which one, so she turned onto Bleecker. Maybe she would remember if she read it. *Mulberry Street—no. Broadway—no. Mercer Street. Is it that one? No.* She kept moving, the wet chill settling into her bones. *Greene Street—no.*

When she came to Wooster Street, she paused.

The corner of Bleecker and Wooster. That was it!

Her joy at figuring out the right corner quickly evaporated as she looked around at the rows of buildings that lined the streets. Which one could it be? She couldn't go knocking on every door. She went up the stairs of the first building she came to and realized that there was a list of names beneath the mailboxes of the people who lived there. Schmidt, Cousins, Morrelli, Anderson. She moved on to the next building. O'Brien. Jamieson. Williams. Leary. Parkman. Again, no Duffy or Grogan. She couldn't find either name on the third building she tried or the fourth or the fifth.

After the sixth building, Sarah gave up hope. She stood at the corner of Bleecker and Wooster and looked around in frustration. She had checked every building anywhere near the corner.

And then she heard a small cough coming from between two nearby buildings. A gaslit lamp beside the door of one of the buildings sent flickering shafts of light into the alley.

Sarah heard the cough yet again and moved toward the sound to investigate. She peered into the dark alley, but in the shadows all she saw were a few trash cans and a large wooden crate. She waited and listened. Nothing. She was about to turn away when she heard the cough again, coming from inside the crate.

Sarah slowly moved to the box and peered into the opening.

Inside, she could just make out a shadowy form lying under a pile of unsold newspapers.

"Tommy?"

The body stirred.

"Red? Is that you?"

Meeting Mr. Duffy

SARAH KNELT BESIDE THE crate and peered inside. Tommy was lying on top of a pile of old newspapers with a layer of other papers covering him like a blanket. He used his wool cap as a pillow. In the dim light from the street, she could see him rubbing his eyes as he struggled to sit up.

"What are you doing out here?" he said.

"I was about to ask you the same thing."

"Come in out of the rain," he said, shuffling aside to make room for her.

Sarah ducked and squeezed herself into the small space beside him.

"Where's your uncle?" he said.

"My uncle?"

"Yeah. Didn't you say you were staying with your uncle?"

"He wasn't really my uncle," she said. "And I think he got arrested."

"Arrested for what?"

"I don't know," Sarah said. "But I can't go back to where I was staying. Or I'll be arrested too."

And then she told him everything. When she finally finished, he shook his head. "I'm really sorry you're in such a tough spot."

"Why are you sleeping out here? What happened to Mr. Duffy?"

"Oh, he's here," he said.

"He is?"

"Come out here, Mr. Duffy."

Sarah heard a small growl from beside Tommy.

"It's okay, boy," Tommy said.

Sarah edged back in surprise as the face of a small mutt popped up from the newspapers beside Tommy and growled at her. He had ragged black hair, with some white around his muzzle, eyes, and on his feet that made him look like he was wearing socks.

"Just let him smell your hand," Tommy said to Sarah.

Sarah extended her hand to the dog, and he gave it a suspicious sniff and then gently licked the backs of her knuckles. Maryk's horseback riding lesson echoed in her head, and she wished that she had a scrap of food to really win him over.

"That's a good boy," Tommy said.

Sarah petted the dog's head. "Why didn't you tell me the truth?"

"I don't like nobody worrying about me," he said. "And Mr. Duffy and I take care of each other. Isn't that right, boy?"

The little dog nuzzled next to Tommy.

"How long have you been sleeping here?" she asked.

"I don't know," he said. "A year. Maybe more. Since my dad died."

"Didn't you say there were rooming houses for boys?"

"I tried staying in one of those places. But my first night a couple of older boys roughed me up and took all my money. I'm better off out here with Mr. Duffy."

"Maybe if we work together, we could afford to stay in a better place," said Sarah. "Somewhere safe."

"I'd like that," he said.

The idea of the partnership sparked new hope in Sarah. Maybe it really would help both of them.

"Let's get a good night's sleep and start fresh in the morning as a team," she said.

She took some papers from the pile and laid under them beside him.

Thunder cracked overhead and the rain fell harder, trickling through the cracks of the crate. Mr. Duffy ducked under the newspapers at the sound of the storm.

"Mr. Duffy hates the thunder," Tommy said. "So do I."

"Do you think he'd like to meet my friend Ivan?"

"Ivan?"

She reached into her coat pocket, pulled out her toy bear, and placed him beside Mr. Duffy.

"This is Ivan. He used to work at a Russian circus before I owned him. He comes from a long line of dancing bears."

"Do dogs and bears get along?" Tommy asked.

"Sure they do," Sarah said. "And Ivan can do all sorts of tricks. Look."

Sarah perched Ivan up on his hind legs and then made him dance in a circle like her father used to do. Mr. Duffy cocked his head and watched with a curious growl. Tommy managed a small smile until there was another loud crack of thunder. Mr. Duffy retreated back under the papers.

"It's hard to sleep with all the noise from the storm," Tommy said.

"When there was thunder back home, my mother always told me to just sing a song in my head to block it out," she said, feeling an ache of sadness.

"I don't know any songs."

"None?"

"Well. No one ever taught me any well enough to remember."

Sarah recalled a lullaby her mother used to sing her when she was a little girl. And the song just came out naturally as if it were her mother's voice singing from inside her body. For the first time, Sarah realized how much her voice was starting to sound like her mother's.

Sleep next to the sun,
Safely tucked away.
Keep each other warm
Until the break of day.

The moon and stars above
Are hiding skies of blue,
So never ever doubt
Your mama's love for you.
No never ever doubt
Your mama's love for you.

Sarah's heart ached to think of her mother, to sing her words and her melody. But remembering also gave her strength. She finished the song and waited for Tommy's reaction. After a moment, she realized that he had fallen asleep. She placed Ivan beside her, spread a few more pages of newspaper over herself, tucked her head under her arm, and closed her eyes.

Girl Newsie

CRASH!

Sarah was startled awake by the screeching noise of metal against stone.

Another crash, and Sarah threw off the newspapers and stepped out of the box. She immediately saw a couple of garbagemen lifting and emptying the trash cans from the alley into a large cart being pulled by a donkey. One of the men saw her and laughed.

"Sorry we woke you, princess," he said as he tossed a trash can back into the alley.

The other man whipped the donkey on the rear with a small riding crop, and the cart moved on. Sarah stepped out of the alley and onto the street. A bright sun shone in a clear blue sky. She stretched her arms over her head and worked the kinks out of her neck.

Her stomach groaned with hunger. It had been a full day since her last meal. She went back over to the crate and knocked on the top.

"Time to wake up," she said.

Mr. Duffy stuck his head out of the opening, stared up at Sarah, and growled.

"You're quite a watchdog, I see," she said. "Come on, Tommy. Let's go make some money to buy ourselves breakfast."

Tommy crawled out of the crate and yawned.

"You've got a deal."

As she watched him, Sarah got an idea.

"May I borrow your hat?"

"Sure. Why?"

He handed her his floppy wool cap, and she placed it on her head, carefully tucking most of her thick red hair beneath it.

"It would probably be better if I didn't stand out so much."

Once her hair was neatly arranged beneath the hat, Sarah and Tommy headed out of the alley and Mr. Duffy moved to follow them.

"No, boy," he said to the dog. "You stay. Someone's gotta guard the crate."

The dog whimpered but returned inside.

They walked east a few blocks until they turned down a wide alley at the back of an industrial building. Several large wagons were parked beside the loading dock stacked with freshly printed newspapers. Two men sat behind a desk with a ledger, doling out newspapers. Dozens of newsies crowded around and waited in a long line to pick up their loads. A few of the other newsies greeted Tommy as they joined the line.

"Who's your girlfriend?"

"She's a tall one."

"Maybe she's his mother!"

"Aw, shut up," Tommy said. "She's my cousin. And she's just working with me."

"Don't you know there ain't no such thing as a girl newsie?" an older boy said with disdain. A few others around him nodded their heads in agreement.

"Well there is now," Tommy snapped. "And if anyone says another word about her, they're gonna answer to me."

"Oh, we're real scared, Tommy," one of them said.

"Don't mind them," Tommy said to Sarah. "They're just jealous." They finally made their way to the front.

"Give me thirty-five," he said.

"Thirty-five?" the dispatcher said. "You usually only take twenty."

"Got some help today," he said.

Tommy handed the man some coins, and the man counted out a stack of papers and handed them over.

Sarah glanced down at the paper and gasped when she saw the front page.

The headline read:

CHINATOWN HUMAN SLAVE RING BUSTED!

Staring up at Sarah were large photographs of Maryk and Mrs. Lee.

Headlines

SARAH GRABBED A PAPER. In the photo Maryk and Mrs. Lee looked disoriented, as if someone had pushed them against a wall to have the picture taken.

"What's the matter, Red?" asked Tommy.

"Hey, get out of the way," one of the other newsies said.

"Yeah, move it along."

Tommy shoved his stack of papers into his bag and then pushed Sarah along, away from the other boys.

She moved to a corner of the alley away from the newsies.

"Sarah?"

"These are my friends," she said, gesturing to the photo.

Tommy grabbed his own paper, and they both read the story.

CHINATOWN HUMAN SLAVE RING BUSTED!

In a daring afternoon raid on Tuesday, the police stormed a building in Chinatown and arrested the owner, Mrs. Bai Lee, along with one of her boarders, Stephen Maryk, and four Chinese girls on suspicion of running a slave ring, in which immigrant girls were used for forced labor or other immoral purposes. Both Maryk, a security guard at the Statue of Liberty, and Lee, the owner of the building, were charged.

"We were tipped off by a source at Maryk's place of employment that he may have been smuggling immigrant girls," arresting officer James Callahan commented. According to the source, the man has a severe drinking problem and had previously been suspended from the job at least once.

As for Lee, she could not explain why four single girls were all living in her building, except to say that she "runs a clean house" and "only wanted to help girls from [her] country." Maryk and Lee deny the charges.

The suspects are being held in the New York House of Detention and will be arraigned tomorrow in New York Criminal Court. Another suspect fled the scene during the raid. Authorities are still looking for the girl, who is described as tall, thin, red-haired, approximately thirteen or fourteen years old. The police are seeking any information leading to the girl's whereabouts. She may also be wanted in connection with other criminal activities.

Tommy looked up at Sarah.

"The tall, thin redhead is you?"

Sarah nodded. She looked around and noticed several of the boys also reading the front page, absorbing all the news so they could shout out the best headlines to draw customers. One of the newsies looked up from reading the article on the front page and squinted at her. He nudged his friend and pointed at the paper and then Sarah.

Sarah lowered her head and hurried away.

Tommy struggled to catch up with her under the weight of the bag. "Wait. Where are you going?"

"I don't know," she said. "I just have to go."

"Hold on," he said, trying to grab her arm. She pulled away.

"No," she said. "Don't you understand? I can't stay with you, Tommy, or you'll get arrested too."

Sarah moved out of the alley. Tommy started after her.

"Sarah! Wait!"

She turned and forcefully held him back by the shoulders.

"Leave me alone," she said. "Just take care of yourself."

Sarah turned and ran. Tommy didn't follow.

Reaching the End

SARAH RAN FOR SEVERAL blocks, still gripping the paper in her hand. Finally she found a quiet street and sat on a stoop to catch her breath. She read and reread the article several times, letting it sink in. Maryk, Mrs. Lee, and the girls might be going to jail, all because of her. They had been strangers, but they'd offered her shelter and kindness.

Sarah felt weighed down by guilt. If she turned herself in, it didn't seem likely that anyone would believe her story—she would just be sent back to her country or arrested too. The newspaper article mentioned that she might be involved in other criminal activities. Could they have possibly found out that she had stolen the egg? In addition to everything else, she was now a thief. She also worried that she had already gotten Tommy into some sort of trouble just for being seen with her.

She wracked her brain for some plan, staring at the sad images of Maryk and Mrs. Lee on the front page. In the back of her mind, she had held on to some slim hope that she could resume her life with them. Living in Chinatown was completely unlike the way she had lived at home, but she had grown to feel comfortable there. Now, everything looked bleak and hopeless.

Two police officers wandered down the street toward where Sarah was sitting, absently twirling their nightsticks and talking with each other. Sarah ducked her head down, shielding herself from their view. She watched them walk by and then moved off in the opposite direction.

She turned down side streets and alleys, not really sure where she was heading, just fleeing from where she had been. Sarah couldn't think of a single place to go, so she kept moving, farther down and around the twisting streets of lower Manhattan. She felt invisible among the crowds of people bustling by her, all with a purpose and a destination except her. Finally, she came to the southwestern edge of the city and recognized the grassy park that abutted the docks along the water of New York Harbor. She spied something shining in the grass by a bench.

As she approached, she discovered a quarter half stuck in the ground. She picked up the coin and placed it in her pocket. At least she could buy herself a hot meal.

She walked along the dock farther south, transfixed as the familiar statue of the Lady came into view shimmering in the distance. Sarah paused and felt her limbs go limp as all the energy drained from her body. The words of the poem rang through her mind: *". . . from her beacon-hand / Glows world-wide welcome. . . ."*

She thought of how the Lady had been a beacon for her and her family, drawing them to America. As she stared at the torch, an idea came to her.

I have to find a way to make people listen to me.

She couldn't run and hide anymore, so she needed to become more visible, to do something to make everyone pay attention to her so she could tell her story and save her friends. If she just let herself disappear or get arrested, no one would care or listen to her. She had to make sure Maryk and Mrs. Lee wouldn't be punished for trying to help her.

She gripped the quarter in her hand and decided that she would use it not to buy food, but for one last ferry ride.

Return to the Lady

SARAH REMOVED TOMMY'S CAP and let the wind sweep back her hair as she stood on the top deck of the ferry that steamed toward the Statue of Liberty. The morning was crisp and clear, with only a few billowy white clouds drifting across the deep blue sky. With the ferry just a few hundred yards away, she could see scores of tourists milling around the statue. Although it had been a couple of weeks since she left the island, she felt as if she had been away for a lifetime.

The boat moored at the dock, and as Sarah stepped onto the island, she took a deep breath of the cool ocean air coming in off the harbor. Roaming the familiar grounds, Sarah felt as if she had come back home. She stopped at the foot of the tree she had hidden in all those nights, then stared at Ellis Island in the distance and the choppy stretch of harbor that separated it from the Lady's island, her mind flashing back to her leap from the ship and swim to safety.

Finally, she moved to the base of the statue and stared up at the Lady and her strong, welcoming face. She thought of the worn postcard she had carried from their village, the first time she and her mother had set eyes on the real thing, and how beautiful she was, and then all the nights she had spent sleeping inside her.

Mother of Exiles, Sarah thought.

Although she hadn't planned to return, she understood that this was her opportunity to say good-bye, to end her journey where it had begun and hopefully help her friends in the process.

She took a deep breath and entered the base. Dozens of people moved up and down the stairwell, their voices echoing in the enormous cavity. She pushed on, higher and higher, until she reached the ladder leading to the torch and climbed up.

Emerging onto the exterior walkway of the torch, she leaned against the railing to catch her breath, sucking the cool salt air into her exhausted lungs and staring out to sea. She remembered watching Maryk do the same all those nights from her hiding spot in the tree. As the waves cascaded into each other and against the shore below, she wondered what Maryk had been staring at all those nights and what he had seen or hoped to see.

Sarah removed Ivan from her pocket and held him up on the railing. She remembered their nights sleeping in the crown, when it had started to feel like her private bedroom. Back then she had felt a sense of adventure and some hope about the future. Now even the Lady felt like a dead end. She looked at Ivan, but she didn't feel like talking to him anymore. He was only a piece of carved wood. She thought about throwing him out into the sea, and even dangled him over the edge, but then pulled her hand back and shoved him into her pocket.

Her mind flooded with everything that had been lost. Her parents, Maryk's wife and child, Bao Yu's father, and all the others from her village and other villages all over the world who had never made it this far.

She spent the afternoon just standing on the torch as tourists came and went to admire the view. No one seemed to notice her. It was as if she didn't exist. Finally the sun began to set over the horizon, a fiery orange ball slowly dimming the sky. She heard the bell ring, announcing the final ferry, and saw the guards encouraging people to make their way toward the dock.

All the other people exited the torch, climbing down the ladder, joining the others who had been in the crown room. But Sarah didn't move.

Eventually the final tourists emerged from the exit at the base of the statue. Two security guards roamed the grounds and made their way toward the entrance of the Lady to make one final sweep. She heard their footsteps getting steadily closer until one of them emerged onto the platform of the torch—a young man with a neatly trimmed black mustache. He regarded her in surprise.

"Miss, what are you doing here?"

She didn't respond.

"Didn't you hear the bell? The last ferry is leaving. I need you to come down now."

Still, Sarah did not reply.

"Miss? Are you all right?"

"I'm not leaving."

"What do you mean?"

"I'm not leaving until I talk to a newspaper reporter."

"A newspaper reporter?" he said, his brow furrowed with confusion. "What are you talking about?"

A moment later, the other security guard emerged onto the platform.

"What's taking you so long, Charlie?"

Sarah stiffened and instinctively drew back as she recognized Maryk's nemesis, Johnson.

His face took on an ugly little smirk. "Well, look what we have here."

Jail

"SHE SAYS SHE WANTS TO TALK to a reporter," the younger guard said.

"Who do you think you are?" Johnson said. "The mayor?"

"You know her?"

Sarah turned away and looked out to sea.

"She's part of that slave ring that Maryk's mixed up in," Johnson said.

"Maryk didn't do anything wrong," she said defiantly.

"Tell it to the judge," Johnson said. "All right, little lady, let's move it."

"I said I'm not going. . . ."

He reached out to grab Sarah's arm and she jerked back, eluding his grasp. Johnson lost his footing.

He scowled. "You want to do this the hard way?"

The younger man stepped forward.

"Please, miss," he said. "There are no reporters out here anyway. Don't make this harder on yourself."

He offered Sarah his hand. She hesitated for a moment, but then put Tommy's cap back on and accepted the man's help. With Johnson positioned in front of her and the younger man behind, they made their way to the door that led from the torch back into the statue. Sarah glanced over her shoulder one more time, saying good-bye to the beautiful view forever, and then ducked inside.

Johnson and his partner led her toward the guardhouse by the dock. The last ferry was moored nearby. Most of the tourists watched from the upper deck, pointing and talking about Sarah.

"There she is," one of them said.

"I heard she wouldn't come down from the torch and they had to drag her out."

"Are they arresting her?"

"What was she doing up there anyway?"

"Where are her parents?"

Sarah was satisfied to see that she had gotten their attention. Now, the word needed to spread. New York city was crawling with reporters looking for stories; she just had to hope word of her arrest would reach some of them.

The two men escorted Sarah into the guardhouse and sat her down at the small wooden table where she had told Maryk her story and eaten the dinner that Mrs. Lee had prepared.

"We've told the ferry captain to send back a special boat for you," Johnson said.

The other guard stepped outside. Johnson crossed his arms and leaned against the door, watching her, as if expecting that she might try to flee. But she had no escape plans.

They waited for over an hour until the police arrived in a small boat. A policeman led Sarah back to the dock.

"Be sure to tell your 'uncle' that I send my regards," Johnson called after her.

Sarah didn't turn to look his way. In fact, she didn't turn to look back at the Lady or the island the entire ride back to Manhattan. She had already said good-bye.

Nearly two hours had passed since Sarah was brought down from the Lady when she got off at the dock in New York. She craned her neck as they approached, hoping to see a crowd waiting for her, but the dock was empty.

Her heart sank as she disembarked and two policemen led her toward a wagon parked on the street nearby.

They were just a few feet away when a round little man wearing a bowler hat ran toward them, carrying a small pad and pen. Another man, thin with a mustache, followed a few paces behind carrying a notebook of his own.

"Miss! Miss! I'm from the *New York World*. I got a tip that you wouldn't come down from the statue. Is that true?"

"No questions, boys," one of the policemen said.

The other reporter stepped in front of them.

"Harry Pinson from the *Times*. Can you tell me what you were doing up in the torch?"

"What are they arresting you for?"

"All right, move along," one of the policemen said, brushing the reporters aside.

The police led Sarah to a horse-drawn wagon just like the one that had hauled off Maryk and Mrs. Lee. Although they didn't put her in handcuffs or chains, Sarah knew she was a prisoner. The men loaded her into the back of the wagon and locked her inside. She could still hear the reporters shouting questions at her through the bars of the wagon as the horses clattered away. She leaned back against the hard wooden wall as they rumbled forward.

At the police station, Sarah told the officer in charge her story. A ruddy-faced man with a shiny bald head, he listened to her intently and made a few notes in a bound book as she talked.

She didn't mention the stolen egg. She felt bad about lying but didn't want to risk getting into deeper trouble.

"What will happen to me?" she asked as she finished.

"I'm not sure," he said. "Trespassing isn't a serious crime. But you're not really a United States citizen, so you're going to have to go before a judge. He'll figure out what to do with you in the morning."

"The morning?" she said with disappointment. She had hoped to be able to explain things right away and help her friends.

"Courts are closed at this hour," he explained. "You'll have to spend the night here."

They gave her a meal of corned beef and boiled potatoes and

then locked her in a small holding cell. She lay on the hard bed, staring up into the darkness and wondering what would become of her. She heard the strange sounds of the building's creaks and groans. A drunken man chattered to himself in the cell next to hers. She tried her best to block out the noise.

For most of her life she had slept in her one-room house in her village, on a mat next to her parents, where she knew every single noise and shadow. In the past several weeks, she had slept in the hull of a ship, a dormitory on Ellis Island, the crown of the Statue of Liberty, a rooming house in Chinatown, and even a box in an alley in the pouring rain. And now here she was expected to find comfort enough to sleep in a jail cell.

Gray streaks of moonlight fell through the bars of a small window near the ceiling, and Sarah wondered if this was the view she would have from now on. She thought of her parents. So much had happened since they both had left her. She felt as if her outer shell had hardened and that she must look very different from when she left her village. She had departed as a girl, a daughter, who was completely tied to her parents' ways. Now, although she was alone, she knew she had become something different, an independent young woman. She was also a prisoner and some sort of criminal, two things she had never imagined she would be. She wondered if her parents would be able to recognize her in heaven if she even got there.

The Girl in the Torch

THE NEXT MORNING SARAH was put in a police wagon and taken to a courthouse a few blocks away. As she emerged from the back of the wagon, a small group of reporters waited for her and shouted questions as she was led up the wide stone stairs to the entrance of the building, which was flanked by a row of massive stone pillars.

Newsboys hawking various morning papers called out their lead stories, most of them having to do with Sarah.

"Extra, extra! Read all about the Statue of Liberty mystery girl!"

"Girl linked to Chinatown slave ring!"

"Girl busted at Statue has her day in court!"

"Get the whole Lady Liberty story here!"

"Sarah!" a familiar voice called.

Sarah scanned the crowd and saw Tommy pushing his way toward her, wearing his full bag of papers slung over his back. He looked strange, and then she realized that it was because he wasn't wearing his cap, which was still on her head.

"Look," he said. "You're famous."

He held up a paper and showed her the front page, which featured the headline THE GIRL IN THE TORCH, accompanied by an illustration of her standing on the torch platform, her long hair blowing in the breeze coming off the ocean.

She stared at the image of herself. Her plan had worked. Now she had everyone's attention.

"Are you all right?" Tommy said. "The paper says you spent the night in jail."

"It wasn't so bad," she said. "And I got a hot meal."

She took off the cap and handed it to him. "Sorry, I forgot to give this back to you."

Tommy took the cap in his hands.

"All right," one of the policemen said. "Move along."

"Good luck in there," Tommy said, adjusting the cap back onto his head.

The policeman gave Sarah a nudge and whisked her inside.

Judge Conklin

THE QUIET IN THE COURTHOUSE surprised Sarah after the noisy bustle in front of the building. She could hear her own footsteps echo against the shiny marble floor as her escorts led her up a grand staircase to a small chamber on the second level.

The police sat her behind a table in a richly appointed office that was lined with dark wood paneling and bookshelves reaching up to the ceiling. A judge sat at the front of the room behind an imposing oak desk covered with books and papers. An American flag hung from the wall behind him, as well as several oil paintings of older men with serious expressions.

The judge had a round red face, white hair, and long bushy sideburns that ran down his cheeks almost to the tip of his chin. Sarah knew he was the one who would hear her story and decide what would happen to her. As soon as the door to the chamber was closed, the judge turned to Sarah.

"My name is Judge Ernest Conklin. Do you speak English?"

"Yes," she said.

"Because I can get a translator to assist you if necessary."

"No," she said with a trace of pride. "I am fluent."

"All right. Do you understand why you are here?"

"You work for the government," she said.

"I am a judge, and it is my job to decide what to do with you. At this point the court is unsure of what criminal laws you may or may not have broken. But we are certain that you are not supposed to be in this country."

Sarah nodded.

"Now, I need to determine the exact nature of your circumstances. And you must tell the whole truth. Lying about anything will only get you in much deeper trouble. So please tell me your story from the beginning."

"The beginning?" she asked. There were so many places to begin.

"How did you get here?" he asked impatiently.

Sarah felt herself freeze up and start to bite her bottom lip in a nervous pulse. But she immediately stopped herself. *You are not a little girl anymore,* she told herself. *Just tell the truth. You have nothing left to lose.*

"I come from a small village," she began.

And then she told him the whole story. She spared no details as she described the massacre in her village, her voyage to America, her mother's death, living in the statue, the kindness of Maryk and Mrs. Lee, and some of the details of her harrowing night on the Bowery. She even confessed to stealing the egg from the tavern.

The only thing she didn't mention was Tommy Grogan. She couldn't risk getting him into trouble.

She finished her story and stood in silence, hoping that the judge would believe her and be understanding.

"Is that all you have to say?" he asked.

Sarah wanted to say more about why she and her mother had come to this country and the promise of America, but she couldn't find the words. The lines of the poem about the Lady echoed in her head and, for the briefest instant, she thought about reciting it. *"Give me your tired, your poor, / Your huddled masses, yearning to breathe free."* Didn't that one sentence explain everything? But she didn't.

"What will happen to me doesn't matter," she said. "But you must believe that Mr. Maryk and Mrs. Lee did nothing but give their kindness to me. And the girls from China, they did nothing wrong either. They work in a factory. They should not be punished because of me. Please."

The judge stared at her for a long moment, rubbing his fingers through his thick sideburns.

"Quite a story," he finally said.

Just then the door to the judge's chamber opened and two guards led in Mrs. Lee and Maryk. His eyes were ringed with deep red bags and it looked like he had not slept. His clothes were creased and dirty and his shirt untucked. Yet as soon as Sarah saw him, her heart rose up in her chest. She wanted to run to him, to see if he was okay, but she knew she had to hold back.

Maryk glanced at Sarah. His eyes narrowed as he stared at her, and she could not read his expression. He was probably furious at her for getting him into so much trouble. His entire face sagged in a defeated frown. She knew that her best friend in America was lost to her.

The Decision

"THIS GIRL IS GOOD GIRL. She did nothing wrong!" Mrs. Lee blurted. "I tell the truth."

"All right, quiet down," the judge said.

"She works in kitchen."

"I said quiet down." The judge banged his gavel on the desk.

Mrs. Lee was about to say more, but the judge pointed his gavel at her and she clamped her mouth shut. Maryk silently stared at the judge.

"Now, I've heard the girl's story," the judge said. "It matches both of yours, so I'm inclined to believe it. Since we confirmed that all the Chinese girls living in your building are employed by the textile firm, you two are free to go."

"Thank you, your honor," Mrs. Lee said with a slight bow.

Maryk didn't move or say anything.

"That still doesn't answer the question of what to do with you," the judge said, turning to Sarah. "While I appreciate the difficulty you've been through, the United States can't let just anybody who suffers an unfortunate circumstance in their own country come live here. Do you understand?"

Sarah nodded.

"You have no blood relatives we could find to sponsor you here. And you do have a living relative in your home country. So I'm afraid I'm going to have to abide by the original ruling of the board at Ellis Island and have you returned to your country to live with your uncle."

Sarah felt her eyes mist over, but she fought back her tears. She didn't want anyone to think of her as a hysterical child. A hollow feeling filled her chest and stomach.

For the first time in days, her mind focused on what life would be like in her home country with her uncle, and every thought made her shudder. She stared down at her feet and nodded.

"I understand," she said.

"Excuse me, your honor." Maryk spoke for the first time.

"Mr. Maryk?"

"What if she had a sponsor?"

Sarah raised her eyes to Maryk.

"The immigration department already tried to find her relations. . . ."

"I know," Maryk said. "That's not what I mean. What if there was someone who was willing to become a guardian for her?"

"And who would that be?"

Maryk hesitated before answering.

"Well . . . me."

Sarah felt her breath catch in her throat as he continued.

"Me and Mrs. Lee, of course. She could live in the building and work for Mrs. Lee at night to earn her keep and then go to school during the day."

"She a good worker." Mrs. Lee nodded.

"I have money saved," Maryk said. "I could pay for whatever sponsorship fees there are."

Overcome, Sarah looked at Maryk. She wanted to run up and give him a hug. But she knew she had to stand where she was. And Maryk wouldn't meet her glance. He kept his eyes on the judge. Sarah turned back to the judge and held her breath. The judge stroked his sideburns thoughtfully.

"Mr. Maryk, I know your intentions are probably good," the judge said. "But you can't expect this court to give custody of a young girl to a middle-aged man with a drinking problem. You are not a blood relative and, frankly, you are not the type of person that we would consider a proper custodian for a child."

"What about me?" Mrs. Lee added.

"Look, this is not how our system works. I would be removed from the bench if I allowed anything like that. And besides, she admitted to stealing. If she were to stay, I would have to have her locked away. This country does not welcome criminals. I'm sorry. My decision is final."

He banged the gavel on his desk.

Deportation Day

FOR TWO DAYS AND NIGHTS SARAH was locked in a damp holding cell in downtown Manhattan, waiting for a ship that was bound to set sail for her old country. Because of her criminal status, she was kept apart from others and was let outside only once a day to stretch her legs in the courtyard of the building. No one was allowed to visit, so she spent her time in silence, counting down the hours until her forced departure and worrying about what life would be like living with Uncle Jossel.

Finally she was transferred by wagon to the New York piers. From there, a ferry would take her back to Ellis Island where the outbound ship would be departing. The sky was heavy and gray, and thick fog rose off the water. A sharp ocean wind blew in from the East River, and the people gathered on the dock to depart or say farewell pulled their hats, scarves, and jackets tighter around themselves and blew into their hands to keep warm.

Sarah was dropped off near the bottom of the gangplank, joining a larger group of ordinary passengers. She moved slowly, her limbs numb and lifeless, knowing there was no way out now. A police officer led her over to another man, who checked her name off a list and then left her to wait with the others. The policeman returned to the wagon and stood talking with two other officers.

The ferryboat was moored in the misty water. The vessel's engine roared to life and the crew prepared to take on passengers and depart. Tommy, Miss Jean, Mrs. Lee, and Maryk stood in a sad clump on the pier, waiting to say their good-byes.

Sarah was cold and tired, but she was glad to see her friends after being alone for two days.

Miss Jean handed her a suitcase made of red-and-black-checkered cloth.

"These are just some of my old things," Miss Jean said. "Most of them should fit, and those that don't right now will after you finish filling out."

"These are your clothes?"

"My *old* clothes. They're yours now. Most of them are out of style anyway. But I figured they won't be where you're from. I also threw in some reading material, so you could practice your English."

Miss Jean opened the suitcase to reveal a well-worn copy of the King James Bible sitting on top of the neatly folded clothes.

"Don't worry. It's one of those editions that has both the New *and* the Old Testaments. Just figured it couldn't hurt for you to get to know Jesus, even if it is just for reading practice."

"Thank you," Sarah said.

Miss Jean gave her a warm hug.

Sarah moved on to Mrs. Lee, who handed her a small bag filled with little tin pots covered with lids.

"I make you lots of rice and noodles, fish cakes, and dried fruit. Good food for you."

"Thank you," Sarah said.

"You remember how to cook like Chinese lady, okay?"

"Okay," Sarah said.

"Bao Yu wanted to be here but could not leave Mrs. Fat. She told me to give this to you."

Mrs. Lee handed her a piece of ginger candy along with a small folded sheet of paper. Sarah opened the note and read the short message, which was handwritten by Bao Yu in the simple but clear letters that Sarah had taught her.

> Thank you. I will not forget you.
> Your friend,
> Bao Yu

Sarah felt a small swell of pride that her student had already learned to write so well.

"Please tell her I will miss her," Sarah said.

Mrs. Lee enveloped her in a quick, strong embrace. Sarah felt her bony frame pull her tightly and then let go.

"You be careful," Mrs. Lee said.

Next in line was Tommy, who wore his floppy wool cap and

had his cloth bag slung around his back.

"I'm gonna miss you, Red."

"Me too," she said.

"So will Mr. Duffy."

Tommy swung his bag forward, and Mr. Duffy popped his head out of the bag and let out a small bark. Sarah stroked the top of his head and he gave her hand a lick.

"Are you two going to be all right?" she said.

"Yeah," he said. "I'm not gonna be sleeping on the street anymore."

"You're not?"

"Mrs. Lee is gonna let me stay at her place."

"As long as he pay rent like everyone else," Mrs. Lee chimed in. "And the dog sleep in backyard. No dogs in my house."

"I'm glad," Sarah said.

"I want you to have this," he said, taking off his cap.

"Really?"

"Something to remember me by."

"Thank you," she said, fitting Tommy's cap onto her head.

"Always looked better on you anyway," he said.

"I want you to have something too," Sarah said.

She reached deep into the pocket of her coat, pulled out Ivan, and placed the toy bear in his hand. Tommy stared at the small treasure.

"Aw, I can't take him from you," he said.

"I want you to have him," she said. "Just don't forget to feed him."

"I won't," Tommy said.

They gave each other a hug good-bye.

Finally Sarah came to Maryk. He was neatly dressed in his brown uniform and hat, clean-shaven, and more clear-eyed than Sarah remembered ever seeing him. He gave her a small sad smile, one of the few times she had seen his face bent in that unfamiliar position.

Maryk's Gift

"YOU LOOK NICE," SHE SAID.

"You've just never seen me in a clean uniform before."

His eyes misted over, and he quickly handed her a brown paper bag. "This is for you."

She looked inside the bag to discover the chess set.

"Thank you," she said.

"And there's something else for you inside," he said.

She looked at him quizzically as she opened the chess set to discover an envelope. She flipped it open and found it filled with a large wad of bills that must have been his life's savings. She gasped in surprise.

"Make sure you keep it somewhere safe, so no one can get at it. Stuff it under your clothes or something."

She closed the chess set and handed the envelope back to him.

"I can't take this."

"Go on," he said, pushing the envelope back to her. "I'd just spend it on whiskey anyway."

"No. I can't. . . ."

"I want you to have it. And you already gave me something."

"I gave something to you?"

He looked her in the eye. "You gave me something to care about."

Sarah glanced down as she felt her face flush and her eyes fill with tears.

"Take it," he said.

Finally she accepted the envelope and tucked it back inside the chess set, which she placed in the bag with Miss Jean's clothes.

"I've got one other thing for you. But don't let anyone see this either."

He glanced around to make sure none of the police officers were watching. Then he reached into the inner pocket of his coat and furtively handed her a small envelope.

"Put it in your pocket," he said.

She did as instructed.

"What is it?"

"A train ticket," he said. "To Oklahoma City."

"I don't understand," she said.

"I've got cousins there, remember? They don't have much. But they'd welcome you like family. I wrote all their contact informa-tion on a piece of paper in there. I already wired them that you might be coming. So they'd be expecting you."

He stared at her.

"You understand what I'm saying?" he said.

"How?" she asked, nervous excitement building inside her.

"Smitty's waiting with a wagon about a block from here, up to the left. He'd get you to the station and make sure you got on the train."

She glanced around at the police milling nearby.

"But how . . . ?"

"We've worked it all out," Maryk said. "A diversion."

He turned toward Mrs. Lee and Miss Jean, who nodded.

"Won't you get in trouble?"

"I don't see how," he said. "You'll just be gone. No one knows I've got Indian cousins anywhere. They'd never find you."

"What if we . . . what if I get caught? Won't they come after me?" She nodded toward the policemen.

"If you get caught, they'll just put you on another boat back to your country. Right? But I don't think that'll happen, because they won't be chasing you too hard. You didn't rob a bank or murder anybody. New York City police have got enough to keep them busy without chasing one girl. Just keep that red hair of yours hidden under that cap and no one'll pay you no mind."

A blast of the boat's horn jarred Sarah.

"All aboard!" one of the crew called.

The other passengers began to move toward the ferry.

"I understand if you don't want to chance it," Maryk said. "You can get on that boat and go. But if you do want to do this, just nod your head and we'll make sure you get on that train."

She stared at him for a long moment, glanced over at Mrs. Lee,

Tommy, and Miss Jean, who were all watching her expectantly. Finally Sarah turned back to Maryk and nodded.

"All right then," he said.

"Will I ever see you again?" she asked.

"Probably not," he said, shaking his head. "Be a mistake for you to ever come back to New York."

They stood before each other for a long moment, until she finally approached and hugged him tightly. At first he was stiff, unsure how to react. She realized it might have been years, maybe decades, since anyone had hugged Maryk. But then he wrapped his enormous arms around her and returned the embrace. His body felt warm and soft, and she rested her head against his chest as he gently patted her hair.

She didn't want to let go.

"You're going to be all right, Androcles," he whispered into her ear.

She looked up at him. "You remember what happened at the end of that story?"

He nodded. "Androcles and the lion are both set free."

"And they go back to their homeland," she said. "Together."

He smiled sadly.

"Yeah. I know. But that's just a story."

"Why can't you come with me?"

"The two of us traveling together would stick out like a sore thumb. Besides, I'm much too slow and old to make that kind of trip," he said with a sad shake of his head. "My place is here now."

Another sharp blast of the boat's horn interrupted them.

"Everyone aboard!" one of the officials shouted.

The crowd noise swelled as the passengers organized themselves into a line near the gangplank. Sarah felt a tremor move through her body and her legs turn to liquid.

One of the policemen approached Sarah. "All right, miss, get with the others. Time to go."

He pushed her into the line. A man collected tickets as the other passengers started up the ramp to the ship. The police officer stood with Sarah to make sure she got on board. The line moved quickly and soon there were just a few people standing between Sarah and the gangplank.

When there was just one person in front of her, Sarah glanced back at Maryk with panic in her eyes. He gave her a nod of encouragement. Then he looked at Mrs. Lee, who subtly nodded back at him.

Suddenly, Mrs. Lee screamed and grabbed her chest.

"Ahhhh," she wailed. "My heart."

Mrs. Lee fell to the ground, with Maryk breaking her fall.

Sarah moved to assist her but then realized that it was all part of the plan.

"Help!" Mrs. Lee shouted.

The police raced to Mrs. Lee as she lay on the ground moaning in fake agony and murmuring in Chinese.

"This lady needs a doctor!" Tommy shouted.

"Clear a path!"

"She's having a heart attack!"

"Give her room!"

As the crowd turned toward Mrs. Lee, Miss Jean grabbed Sarah by the elbow and pulled her away from the dock.

"Don't look back," Miss Jean said. "Just act naturally. Like we're normal folks taking a walk."

Sarah felt the adrenaline rushing in her chest as they walked away. She carried the suitcase in one hand and nervously gripped the train ticket in her pocket with the other, squeezing the envelope until her knuckles turned white. She and Miss Jean wove through the crowd.

Sarah wanted to look back and see her friends one more time, but she knew she couldn't risk it. So she just walked on. Her pace quickened to keep up with Miss Jean's. The noise of the crowd began to recede, and the boat's horn blasted again.

One Regret

MISS JEAN LED SARAH THROUGH the crowd to the main street and turned left. In the distance, Smitty's wagon came into view.

"There he is," Miss Jean said.

Smitty sat holding the reins of a one-horse dray, ready to go. As they approached, the ship's horn sounded again. The horse bucked and whinnied loudly.

"Whoa, boy," Smitty said.

But the horse reared up on its hind legs and cried out again. Sarah and Miss Jean both recoiled and took a step back. Smitty tried to calm the animal, but it wouldn't settle down.

"Calm that beast," Miss Jean said.

"I'm trying!" he said.

Fear gripped Sarah for a moment, but then she remembered what Maryk had taught her.

"Do you have a carrot or anything to eat?" she called to Smitty.

"I've got an apple."

"Throw it to me," she said.

Smitty reached into his pocket and tossed Sarah an apple.

The horse eyed Sarah warily as she approached from the left with the apple in her palm.

"It's okay," she said.

She looked into the horse's eyes and placed a hand on his neck and shoulder.

"Good boy," she said.

She carefully extended her hand. The horse snatched the apple from her palm and chewed it with his big yellow teeth.

Sarah rubbed his neck and exhaled a breath into his nostrils. The horse calmed under her touch.

"Come on, girl," Smitty said. "Gotta get a move on."

Smitty offered Sarah his hand, and he hauled her up to the seat beside him.

"Good luck, child," Miss Jean said. "And God bless you."

"Thank you," Sarah said.

"C'mon, boy," Smitty called to the horse. "Giddyup."

Smitty snapped the reins, and the horse moved off away from the pier.

In that moment, Sarah didn't doubt that she had to seize this chance. She didn't fear getting caught. And she certainly wasn't sorry that she would not be going back to her homeland. She just wished that she had told Maryk she loved him when she had the chance.

Going West

FOR THREE DAYS, SARAH SAT in a window seat and watched the scenery spin by in a mad blur. Past cities, forests, rivers, farmland, hills, plains, and dozens and dozens of towns—she could barely keep track of all the different sights that danced beside the railroad tracks on her journey west. She enjoyed the constant rumble of the train and the aching whistle of the locomotive as it blew through station after station.

Sarah barely allowed herself to sleep, not wanting to miss anything. The vastness of the country shocked and excited her, and she swore to herself that she would remember it all. She carefully parceled out the food Mrs. Lee had prepared for her, eating a small portion of rice and vegetables each day to make it last until she reached Oklahoma.

Every so often she'd take out her father's tailoring scissors, which she still carried in the inner pocket of her coat. She held them up to the window and let the sun glint off the shiny blades. Something about holding the scissors gave her a sense of hope about the future.

She put the scissors back in her pocket and thought of her parents. If only they could see her now. She felt so different from the little girl who had left their village. Sarah wondered if they would have made the same choice to escape. Somehow she doubted it, and that thought made her feel an unexpected sense of pride and independence.

She also thought about Maryk and all he had sacrificed for her. She was determined to make him proud.

A train conductor appeared at the head of the car and removed a large silver watch attached to a chain from the pocket of his vest.

"All right, folks, forty minutes to Oklahoma City," he called out. "Oklahoma City will be our next stop."

Sarah leaned back in her seat and felt her heart beat in time with the rhythm of the train. She gazed out the window and with each mile felt hope and anticipation for what her new life might bring.

Fifteen Years Later

The Boy in the Torch

THE BOY STOMPED UP the stairs, ahead of his mother and father, delighting in the clanging echo his footsteps made in the statue's interior. When he reached the landing, he scrambled up the ladder and burst out into the blinding daylight on the platform of the torch.

"Whoa!" The boy gasped. His seven-year-old eyes had never seen anything so magnificent. Gulls squawked in the brilliant blue sky overhead as the boy climbed up on the railing and looked around at the steamships and sailboats moving in and out of the harbor. His red hair shone in the sunlight.

His mother and father finally emerged onto the platform.

"Get away from the edge!" Sarah called.

The boy hesitated.

"You heard me, Maryk," she said. "Get down from there!"

"Listen to your mother," the man said, pulling his son back down to the platform.

The three of them looked out at the view together without

speaking for a few moments. The little boy removed a small toy lion from the pocket of his jacket and placed it on the railing so it could look out at the view, just as his mother had years before. The boy finally broke the silence.

"Did you really live here?"

"Right down there," Sarah said, turning and pointing to the crown, nodding her head.

"And the man that I'm named for. He lived here too?"

"No. He worked here."

"How come he never came to visit you?"

"I think he wanted to. But as he got older, it got harder and harder for him to travel. I finally convinced him to come out right around the time your father and I got married. I'd asked him to walk me down the aisle. He bought a train ticket and everything. But then . . ." Sarah's voice got caught in her throat.

Her husband took her hand.

"But then he got sick and just couldn't make the journey," she said. "A little while later his heart gave out. Maybe it was just too big."

Sarah's eyes misted over as she looked back out into the harbor. "But before I ever met him, he'd come up here every night and look out to sea just like we're doing now."

"At night? But he couldn't really see much, could he?"

"No," Sarah said. "Not really."

"Then what was he looking for?"

Sarah took a deep breath, and a small smile curled her lips.

"Sometimes I think he must have been looking for me."

Author's Note

THIS IS A WORK OF FICTION. In fact, the first draft of this novel was written without any reference to Sarah's country of origin or religion, as I wanted the story to feel as universal as possible. However, I later decided to base in her in a reality similar to my own family history to make the story more realistic and grounded in true history.

Although I tried to create an authentic feeling of the time and place of turn-of-the-century New York, there were some instances in which I knowingly diverged from historical fact for dramatic effect. For instance, an immigrant child like Sarah who was orphaned on Ellis Island would not have been sent back to her home country, but rather returned to the port of origin of the ship that brought her. If that had happened, Sarah's fate might have been even worse than if she had been returned to her uncle. And there were Jewish-American agencies that often aided immigrant children in distress.

As Miss Jean notes to Sarah, women in Chinatown were extremely rare. After the Chinese Exclusion Act of 1882, Chinese immigrants were not allowed to become citizens; and before then, only men were granted access to the United States to work. The few Chinese women who did inhabit the neighborhood were typically the spouses or children of merchants, although there were also young Chinese women being illegally exploited or enslaved in some way.

The geography and population of what is now known as Liberty Island varied greatly over the years, but it was likely never left only in the care of a single night watchman.

Note on the Origins
of the Story

LIKE SARAH'S FATHER, MY great-grandfather was a buttonhole maker. When he emigrated from Russia, he had almost no money or worldly possessions, but he did have his tailoring skills and one fine pair of scissors. Those scissors are still a precious family heirloom. It strikes me as nothing short of miraculous that he was able to forge a life for himself and his family with such meager beginnings.

A few years ago, I came across the fact that the very first person ever processed at the Federal Immigration Center on Ellis Island in 1892 was a fifteen-year-old girl from Ireland named Annie Moore. She traveled to America with her two younger brothers to be reunited with their parents, who were already living in New York. I marveled at the risks and dangers of Annie's journey, and part of me wondered what would have happened to her if her parents had died or could not be found once she arrived.

Later, I read a biography of the singer Dean Martin, who was the son of Italian American immigrants. The author of the book,

Nick Tosches, wrote about how important the Statue of Liberty was as a symbol to Italian immigrants, and I realized that this was true of so many different ethnic and religious groups. Tosches also quoted the Emma Lazarus poem, "The New Colossus," and I was arrested by the line describing the statue as the "Mother of Exiles." It was in that moment that I decided to write a story about an immigrant girl who loses her mother and lives inside the Statue of Liberty, so the monument becomes almost like a surrogate mother.

On the following pages I've included notes on some of the sources I used when writing the book as well as a timeline of the Statue of Liberty, Ellis Island, and U.S. immigration policy.

Sources

I ALWAYS READ AS many history books as I can when research-
ing a novel set in the past. However, I often find that some of
the most interesting sources of insight and inspiration come from
unexpected places. Here are a few that I found most helpful when
writing about the immigrant experience and New York City at
the turn of the twentieth century.

PHOTOGRAPHY—Photography and photojournalism were
booming in the early 1900s. Jacob Riis published a book called
How the Other Half Lives that chronicled life in the slums of New
York. It features incredible photographs of real immigrants, many
of them children, who lived in poverty on the streets and in tene-
ments. Another photographer at the time, named Lewis Hine,
captured vivid images of immigrants on Ellis Island and child
laborers around the city and the county.

MUSIC—The ragtime music of Scott Joplin makes the feel
and rhythm of early-twentieth-century New York come alive.

Although written more than one hundred years ago, songs like "The Maple Leaf Rag" and "The Entertainer" are still popular today. Many songs of old New York still exist that were written about the city at the time. These tunes evoke that era and place with both their melodies and lyrics, including "Sidewalks of New York," "Chinatown, My Chinatown," and "The Bowery," which I quoted in the book.

NEW YORK CITY—Perhaps the most exciting way to experience the history of New York is to visit the sites themselves. In addition to the Statue of Liberty and Ellis Island, there are many other places to explore that make the past come alive. The Lower East Side Tenement Museum gives you a wonderful sense of what everyday life was like for poor people living in the city. That museum is just a short walk from Chinatown, the Brooklyn Bridge, and the Bowery, where Sarah had some of her adventures. If you can't visit New York, there are plenty of videos of all of these places on YouTube.

FAMILY—As I mentioned earlier, the origins of this story came from the story of my own great-grandfather's life and his buttonhole-making scissors. Whether they arrived two hundred years ago or last week, your family will likely have their own immigration story that is filled with risks, adventure, sacrifice, and dreams of a better life in America. Perhaps one of your relatives even carried a postcard of the Statue of Liberty on the journey.

A Time Line of the Statue of Liberty, Ellis Island, and United States Immigration Policy

1776

A New York merchant named Samuel Ellis owns an island in New York Harbor previously known as Gull Island, Oyster Island, Dyre's Island, Bucking, and Gibbet Island. He runs a tavern on the island that is popular with fishermen.

1865

A Frenchman named Edouard de Laboulaye proposes that France give a statue representing liberty as a gift to the United States to celebrate its centennial. He believes the gift will help promote the ideals of democracy in his own country.

1870

French sculptor Auguste Bartholdi begins designing the Statue of Liberty.

1882

President Chester A. Arthur signs the Chinese Exclusion Act, prohibiting all immigration of Chinese laborers.

1883

Emma Lazarus composes the poem "The New Colossus" as part of a fund-raising effort for the Statue of Liberty.

1885

The Statue of Liberty is shipped from France to the United States in pieces, but must be placed in storage for a year to await the completion of the pedestal.

1886

The pedestal and statue are completed. It is formally unveiled at a ceremony on Bedloe's Island.

1890

The federal government begins setting up an immigration station on Ellis Island.

1891

The Immigration Act establishes the first set of comprehensive laws relating to immigration control and the deportation of illegal aliens.

1892

The Ellis Island Federal Immigration Station opens. The first immigrant processed there is a fifteen-year-old girl from Ireland named Annie Moore. Some 450,000 immigrants are processed there that first year.

1900

Ellis Island's Main Immigration Building opens and can receive 5,000 immigrants per day.

1903

Emma Lazarus's poem "The New Colossus" is inscribed on a plaque that is placed at the base of the statue.

1907

This is the peak year of immigration through Ellis Island, with more than a million immigrants processed.

1921

The U.S. Congress passes the Emergency Quota Act, which sets a yearly limit on the number of immigrants from any country to 3 percent of the number of people from that country already living in the United States as of 1910.

1924

President Calvin Coolidge declares the Statue of Liberty a national monument.

The Immigration and Naturalization Act establishes the first numeric limits on the number of immigrants to the United States.

The U.S. Border Patrol is established.

1939–1945

During World War II, Ellis Island is used as a detention and deportation center for "alien enemies." More than 7,000 Japanese, Germans, and Italians are detained during this time.

1940

The Alien Registration Act requires registration of all "aliens" living in the United States.

1954

Ellis Island is closed as a federal facility.

1956

Bedloe's Island is officially renamed Liberty Island.

1965

President Lyndon Johnson signs the Immigration Act that eliminates nationality, race, or creed as a basis for admittance to the United States.

President Lyndon Johnson places Ellis Island under the care of the National Parks Service.

1976

Ellis Island opens to tourists.

1984–1986

The Statue of Liberty undergoes a major renovation.

1986

The Statue of Liberty celebrates its centennial with a massive celebration.

1990

The Ellis Island Immigration Museum opens.

2001

After the attacks of 9/11, the Statue of Liberty is closed for security reasons. The pedestal does not reopen until 2004 and the crown does not reopen until 2009.

Acknowledgments

FIRST I WANT TO thank my wonderful editor, Kristin Daly Rens, who has been an invaluable collaborator throughout the entire creative process.

In addition to handling the business side of the business for me, my agent Maria Massie is a critical reader and a dear friend. Kassie Evashevski is my stalwart representative on the west coast.

My friend Barbara Clews offered me great insights into the world of horses and helped to guide the writing of the equine sections of the story. I'd also like to thank Bridget Morrison, who is always supportive and unusually upbeat about everything. Martin Curland remains one of my most trusted, honest, and insightful early readers.

I'd also like to thank Peter Glassman for generously replacing my lucky Books of Wonder coffee mug just in the nick of time.

My parents, Arthur and Judy Sharenow, continue to be my loudest and proudest supporters. I'd also like to thank my in-laws, Harvey and Cindy Creem, for all their love and support.

I want to specially acknowledge my father-in-law. This novel is about a man who helps save a girl who emerges from the sea. While I was in the process of writing this book, Harvey saved my daughter Olivia from drowning. Our gratitude for his heroism on that day can never be properly expressed. Yet it has also become clear to me that if not for his actions, I never would have finished this particular story.

This book is dedicated to my girls, Annabelle and Olivia, who are the greatest beacons of light in my life. And finally, I want to thank my wife, Stacey, who will always be my first and most important reader.